I0724036

Contents

Heading For Sunset

and other stories

by
Bryan Darby

© 2022

Inquiries and Book Orders should be addressed to:

Great Writers Media
Email: info@greatwritersmedia.com
Phone: 877-600-5469

ISBN: 978-1-960605-66-5 (sc)
ISBN: 978-1-960605-67-2 (ebk)

Contents

Heading for Sunset

August had come in hot, and the haze that still rose from the road made the lights of the small town flicker as they grew steadily closer. The long drive had started to take its toll fifty miles back and I winced as I turned the wheel and slid to a halt beneath a neon sign that spluttered back and forth between 'Vacancy' and 'No Vacancy'.

The big guy behind the desk slid a key in my direction without looking up from his paper.

"Top of the stairs, first right. Seven-fifty up front. Shower's extra."

I pushed the key back.

"I'll take the shower."

The guy blocked it.

"Same room, Mac. That'll be eight even."

"How'd you know if I'd showered anyways?"

He thumbed towards a grubby sign behind him. It read 'In God we trust. All others pay!'.

"You ain't heard the plumbing, mister."

The room was cold. I turned on the radiator. It ticked for several minutes before settling to a continuous gurgling as the air filled with the odor of long-dead cheroots and stale sweat.

I went back down to the desk.

"Where's the best place to eat?" I asked.

"Best? Worst? Ain't but one. End of the block. Millie's joint."

I could hardly have missed it. 'BEST STEAK IN TOWN' was scrawled across the grimy window.

Most of the tables were piled high with chairs and the place had the air of a morgue after closing time. A girl with mousy hair looked up and smiled as I entered.

A scowling, thickset woman I took to be Millie emerged from a kitchen I preferred not to contemplate.

"What's it to be, mister?" The cigarette that clung to her thick lips showered ash with each word.

I settled for steak.

"Steak's Monday. Today's Wednesday. Special's hash."

I had a two-hundred-mile appetite.

"Fine," I said, and made to take down a chair from one of the tables.

"Too grand to share, mister?" Millie rasped.

I looked at the mousy girl and shrugged. She smiled. I pulled out a chair and sat down.

"Hi. I'm Don."

"Hi, Don. I'm Jeane..." She hesitated. Then: "With an 'e'."

The voice was breathy and quiet.

"Well, hi there. Jeane-with-an-'e'. You from round here?"

"No. Just passing through. My connection

to LA is at seven tomorrow morning."

In the harsh light of the bare bulbs, she had a kind of girl-next-door quality but, with the right makeover, she could be every kind of beautiful.

"LA, huh? My office is in Hollywood. Sunset and Vine."

For a moment, the smile lost its warmth, and she sucked in her top lip, thrusting her lower jaw forward challengingly.

"You going to hand me that tired old line about being a movie director?"

That surprised me. In my business, one hint that you work for a major picture corporation and the dames are yours for the taking. This one didn't jump so easily.

"No. Not a director. But it's not a line and I do work for the studios."

I placed a deck of calling cards on the table.

"That's me. Don Scott, Talent Scout."

"Have you spotted anyone I might recognize, Mr Scott?"

Now it was 'Mr Scott'. I could feel my fur getting rubbed the wrong way.

"Great talent is hard to come by. Anyways, it's early days yet."

"Which is your way of saying you haven't?"

I slipped the cards back in my pocket. Jeez! I was going places and I wasn't about to get sandbagged by some mousy broad. Nossir!

Just then, Millie barged out of the kitchen and slapped a dish of hash in front of me with a rasping "Enjoy!"

The distraction gave me time to think.

"You can look out for Candy O'Connor, Lee-Anne Lambert, Drew Dodds. They'll all be household names by this time next year."

Jeane-with-an-'e' just smiled.

"Okay," I said, "but... how about you?"

She ignored the question.

"They all have made-up names. No-one gives their kids names like that."

"The studios are hot on alliterative names. They're all the rage. Greta Garbo, Claudette Colbert, Deanna Durbin, Roy Rogers. They're easy to remember and they look good in lights."

She laughed. "Well, like they say... I guess that's show business."

I smiled and studied her closely for a few moments.

"And you really don't have Hollywood in those baby-blues? Hell, with your looks, you could be a sensation. Yeah! But... blonde. Real blonde. Jean Harlow blonde. I mean it. Now, *that's* how I see you."

For once I was being sincere. I hoped it sounded that way.

She laughed again. A different kind of laugh.

She picked up her coffee cup and stared at me across the rim.

"Blonde? Me? Jeepers, no! I'd never go *that* blonde. Not for anything."

"It didn't do Jean Harlow any harm," I enthused.

"You know," Jeane-with-an-'e' put down her empty coffee cup and ran the tip of one carefully manicured finger round the rim. "When I was little, she was my favorite, and she sure did have beautiful hair. But..." Her eyes twinkled. "She also had different initials. 'J' and 'H'. I guess they didn't go for alliteration in those days."

This kid's complacency was getting to me. With the war in Europe just over, the streets of LA would be full of young broads just begging for a screen test and some were gonna make it big. I was all set. I sure as hell didn't have the time to persuade her. I changed the subject.

We walked back to the lodging house where she had a room along from mine.

I set the radio alarm for six-thirty, turned out the light and just lay there for a while. My future was all mapped out. I knew exactly where I was going and how I was going to get there. As the long drive finally started to have its way, my last thoughts were of Jeane-with-an-'e'.

Morning came with a dramatic voice

reporting on the explosion of something called an atom bomb at Alamogordo a couple weeks back. I muttered something about dropping one on Tokyo and tuned to a station playing Glenn Miller.

I packed my grip, checked that I had everything I came with and went to look for some breakfast.

Millie's was closed. I went back to the lodging house and rang the bell. The big guy came out pulling on a grubby sweat shirt.

"Kitchen's closed," he growled.

The sun was already warm. I put the top down and backed out into the road. In the distance, a solitary figure waited at the bus stop. It was unmistakably Jeane-with-an-'e'.

I drew in alongside and opened the door. She reached down to pick up her valise, allowing me a tantalizing glimpse of the delights that lay beneath her loose-fitting dress. She noticed my admiring glance and hesitated, likely wondering what strings might be attached. Then she smiled, tossed the valise in back and slid in beside me.

We drove in silence for a while with the sun warming our backs. She relaxed, eyes closed, allowing the wind to stream through her shoulder-length hair and occasionally smoothing her dress down to prevent it blowing above her knees.

It must have been a half hour before the silence got to me.

"You really should try modeling, you know."

From the tail of my eye, I saw her lips curve into a smile.

"Uh-ha."

I tried again when we stopped off to eat.

An hour later we were on our way again.

"When we get to LA, just walk into an agency. Any agency. What's to lose? You married?"

I don't know what made me ask, but I knew she'd heard me.

There was no response. I took that to mean 'yes' and fell silent again.

Maybe she was running away from her old man. Maybe he beat her. Maybe she'd found another guy someplace. Maybe...

Hell! I'd only met her last night and here I was acting like I should care.

How old could she be? Twenty? Nineteen? I just couldn't see her tied to a kitchen sink for the rest of her life.

The conversation lapsed into a companionable silence again till the outskirts of LA came into view. It wasn't long before we turned onto Wilshire Boulevard and I drew up outside a hotel with a sign pointing to a model agency inside.

I switched off the engine.

"You could do a heck of a lot worse."

Jeane-with-an-'e' started to open the door then turned and asked if I had anything to write on.

I fished a crumpled piece of paper from my vest pocket and handed her my fountain pen.

She scribbled for several seconds, blew on the paper and waved it to dry the ink then handed the pen back. As I slipped it in my pocket, she leaned across and gave me a quick peek on the cheek, unwound herself onto the sidewalk and snapped the door shut.

"Thanks, Don," she breathed, and dropped the paper on the seat.

I fired up the Chevy and drew away with a momentary regret that I'd never hear that breathy voice again. I raised my hand in a cheery wave.

In the rear-view mirror. I saw her return the wave, holding it for a moment before picking up her valise and going into the hotel.

Turning onto La Cienega, I glanced at the paper fluttering on the seat.

Sure, I'd found her attractive. Jeez! Most guys would. But, in my professional opinion, she just didn't have what it takes. There were a million dames out there who needed me. Dames with talent and ambition. Guys, too. They wanted fame. I wanted fortune.

Turning onto Rossmore, I eased back in my

seat. It had been a long trip.

As I crossed Melrose onto Vine, heading for Sunset, I picked up the paper and glanced at it then held it up and let the wind take it.

As it fluttered from my fingers, I knew that Jeane-with-an-'e' had made a connection somewhere deep down inside. Maybe it was her naivety and that 'girl-next-door' innocence. Whatever, it had touched me more deeply than I cared to contemplate. But, hey! I just didn't have the time to get that close to anybody. Not right now.

I tried to brush aside the memory of that breathy voice and the subtle aroma of her presence as I slid into my usual space in the parking lot in back of the office.

I took the elevator up to the fourth floor, tossed my grip into the corner of the office and sat at the desk. After a few minutes. I ratcheted a new sheet of paper into the machine and began to type.

As I worked, the sky slowly reddened. I swiveled round and took in the familiar scene of the street below filled with workers streaming from their offices and lights began to snap on all along the block opposite.

Switching on my desk lamp, I worked on as the evening progressed into a blazing sunset.

Traffic noise softened as the pace of the city slowed and, again, my thoughts began drifting towards that indefinable something that was Jeane-with-an-'e'.

I dropped my work folder in the tray ready for the secretarial agency to pick up in the morning and decided to call it a day.

It was late the next afternoon when Marlene called from the agency. She wanted to know the significance of the name that cropped up several times in the documents that I had sent. I told her it was a character in a script I was working on and said to ignore it. I hung up and decided to call it a day.

It took the whole weekend and a couple bottles of Bourbon trying, unsuccessfully, to work her out of my system.

But, unless someone out there was looking for a mousy broad with a great figure and a quiet voice, one thing was for certain sure.

Norma Jeane Dougherty was never going to see *her* name up in lights. Nossir! ◆

Last Wish

From the moment that Arthur Grant's feet had touched the bedroom carpet, he knew it was going to be one of those days. The mood had gathered momentum when he spilled his morning tea into his lap.

Hastily changing, he scooped the morning's mail into his pocket and splashed to the bus stop just in time to see his bus disappearing into the rain-sodden distance.

"Oh, Ratbag!" he muttered, remembering Dr Crawford's warning. Only yesterday the bus had been delayed, making Arthur late for the first time in seven years. The resulting admonishment had ended with a pointed warning not to let it happen again — and 'Crabby' Crawford was not a man to threaten lightly. Surprisingly, when Arthur let himself into the laboratory at twenty-seven minutes past eight, Crawford had not yet arrived. Usually they would already be hard at work when the other departments started at nine o'clock.

Changing into a white dust coat. Arthur opened a fume cabinet and took out a flask containing a pink liquid. As he placed it gently on his workbench his arm jogged a retort full of blue crystals. In his haste to grab it, the precious flask went flying. They hit the floor simultaneously.

"Oh, Ratbag!" Arthur cursed in annoyance as a cloud of mauve vapour mushroomed upwards.

"Yeah?"

Arthur looked around to see who had spoken.

"Oh yeah! 'Ang about a bit, mate," the voice went on. There was a sound of fingers snapping. "There! That better?"

Arthur gaped.

Where the column of fumes had been stood a paunchy figure wearing a turban and voluminous satin pantaloons. Long, curling slippers encased his feet and gold bangles adorning his arms shone dully in the fluorescent lighting. His face wore a large, friendly grin.

"W-who are you?" stammered Arthur, thinking he'd been overcome by the fumes.

"Ratbag," said the newcomer, airily. "Well, summat like that. Near enough, anyway. Traditional, that is. Full of Eastern Promise, you might say. Anyway, I can't hang about 'ere all day, mate, so name it an' it's yours.

"Oh, but I didn't actually..." Arthur suddenly remembered his outburst.

"Look, Chief," grinned the other. "It don't make no odds to me what you 'actually'. It's annuver of them traditions. You're the one what called me up, so you're the one what gets the wishes. Right? Free of 'em, like in the old days. Get me?"

"I wish I knew what you were talking about."

Ratbag solemnly raised a hand and snapped his fingers.

"Right'o! There you go, then. That's one. What's next?"

Instantly, Arthur knew how the combination of chemicals had produced the genie and how the catalytic action of air had produced genies from ancient brass bottles in the legends of Arabian Nights. But, beyond any doubt whatsoever, he knew that this was really happening.

"It's a bit parky in 'ere, ain't it."

The genie's bangles jingled as he rubbed his bare arms.

"Well, what do you expect?" Arthur chuckled. "You'd be a lot warmer back home in Persia."

Ratbag looked quizzical.

"What you on about? British, I am, Squire. This is Dalston, innit?"

With another snap of his fingers he was dressed in a navy-blue donkey-jacket, black corduroy trousers and heavy hobnailed boots.

"There! Okay? Now, about them uvver two wishes. What's it going to be, then? Money?

Power? Birds?"

"Well, a decent bit of cash wouldn't go amiss, but it would have to be tax free and legal."

Snap! Somehow, Arthur knew that he had got his wish.

"Two down, one to go," chanted Ratbag.

"All right. Don't rush me."

Pausing to consider the possibilities of this one last wish, Arthur thought about the genie's other suggestions.

Power? No, he'd never had any strong aspirations in that direction. That left one possibility. Here he was, thirty-six and still single. Innate shyness with the opposite sex had, until now, deprived Arthur of any opportunity for romance.

"Why not?"

He pictured a girl he'd seen once or twice in the High Street. If he could just...

"I wish..."

Snap!

Ratbag's grin widened. With a friendly 'thumbs up', he vanished in a suffocating cloud of mauve vapour. Arthur choked and the room spun...

Arthur felt cool sheets through pyjamas.

The air was filled with the smell of antiseptic and clean, white hospital linen.

Firm, gentle hands straightened the covers. He opened his eyes. It was the girl from the High Street. She was in the uniform of a ward sister.

"Hello," she smiled. "Feeling better?"

She explained how Arthur had been overcome by fumes and, as no harm had been done, he would be discharged later in the day but she added that he should rest for now.

As she left the ward, Arthur realised that, except for his coincidental meeting with the Sister, there was nothing to substantiate his fast-fading dream. He looked around the small, obviously private, ward.

Two crumpled letters lay on the bedside cabinet. One, bearing the Company's crest, explained that Crawford had been posted to another branch at short notice and that, with immediate effect, Arthur was now head of the department.

He could have shouted for joy.

The Sister returned just as he opened the other envelope. He scanned the contents and immediately felt like bursting into song, but restrained himself at the realisation that it might harm his next move.

"Sister... will you have dinner with me tonight?" There, he'd said it.

"Thank you. I'd love to, Dr Grant. Something to celebrate?"

"A big win on the Premium Bonds and

promotion at work. And, to cap it all, I'll never have to clap eyes on Old Crabby again."

"Old Crabby?"

"Yes. My boss, Dr Crawford. He's a real pain..."

"That's a bit harsh, don't you think? Surely he's not as bad as all that."

Arthur sniggered.

"Oh yeah? You don't know him."

"Well, actually, I do. I'm Angela. Angela Crawford. Daddy's a real softy when you get to know him. And he speaks very highly of you."

Arthur suddenly felt his world starting to collapse around him.

Angela smiled. "Perhaps I should have introduced myself before you asked me out."

She took the water jug from the bedside cabinet and, throwing a cheeky grin back over her shoulder, headed for the door.

"But as long as you don't mind being seen out with Old Crabby's daughter, I'm still game..."

The door swung shut behind her.

"Oh. Ratbag!" Arthur cursed emphatically.

Out of nowhere, a jovial chuckle rippled around the room.

"Nah! Not this time, Sport. This time, you're on your own!" ◆

First Day

"And how did my little man enjoy his first day at his new school?"

Pauline could see from the look on Frankie's face that he hadn't enjoyed it one bit. Hanging his head, he plodded dramatically across the room and slumped untidily onto the settee before replying.

"They made fun of me."

Pauline sat beside him, putting a comforting arm around him.

"It'll be better tomorrow. All children pick on the odd one out. After all, you *are* the new boy. They don't know you. You'll soon settle in and, when they do get to know you, I'm sure they'll change. Oh..."

She rapidly changed the subject in an effort to take his mind off his first-day blues.

"How on earth did you manage to get so much mud over your lovely new trousers?"

"The others did it." Frankie's expression saddened. "They said I wasn't like them because they all wear the school uniform and that's got short trousers. I tried to tell them that mine was being made to measure and they started calling me names."

A tear began to well up in his eye.

"Mummy, what is a... a snob?"

Pauline sighed with relief.

"Oh, that's nothing. That's only them being jealous..."

"Well, that's what they called me and that's when they started rolling me in the mud. They said that I looked like something that had been dug up, so I should be buried again."

Tears were now flowing freely.

"But they didn't actually hurt you did they? I mean... you're all right otherwise?"

Frankie sniffed and pulled a large, grubby hankie from his tunic pocket and blew loudly into it.

"No, I'm all right. You know I don't feel pain since the operation. But I have got feelings, Mummy. I'm a still a human being just like them, aren't I?"

"You'll feel better after a good meal."

Pauline got up and went into the kitchen.

Supper over, they sat down to watch telly.

"You know, Frankie." said Pauline, "If your father could see you now he'd be really proud of you."

Frankie picked up the remote control from the floor and smiled up at her in that special way she had grown to love.

"Thank you, Mummy."

Pauline snuggled down and held tight to Frankie's hand. Who knows what talent was locked in those delicate fingers. Brain surgeon? Artist? Violinist, perhaps?

Oh, how she missed Victor. So much time had passed since she had last seen him. Every night, she prayed that somewhere out there he was still thinking about her and Frankie.

Pauline had never been able to bring herself to believe that Victor had thought their passionate affair was just a holiday romance. After all, he had asked her to bring Frankie back with her... to adopt him... with all the attendant paperwork and legal problems and expense. But they'd be all right. Of that she was sure.

Several minutes passed in relative silence, then Frankie shifted his position and looked up at her.

"Mummy," he said pensively, "why don't the other boys have a bolt through their neck, like me?" ♦

<u>Ambition</u>

Have you ever wondered what it's like to be a Fairy? You might think it's all a wave of the wand and little rays of sunshine, but it's not.

Oh. no!

Now, don't get me wrong. I'm not unhappy. But I *can* remember happier days, when I was small.

Okay, I know you'd think I was small anyway because I'm only seven-and-a-half centimetres tall. That may only be three inches in real money, but that's quite a bit above average for a Fairy.

What I mean is... when I was *very* small. In the days when my Mum used to tuck me up in my little acorn-cap bed.

She used to tell me stories about Humans. Of course, I didn't believe in *them* any more than you probably believe in us.

Well, not until I started to grow up, that is.

We used to live out in the middle of a big meadow, you see.

We believed in *cows.* Of course we did. We spent most of our time trying not to get trodden on by them. And there were badgers. And hedgehogs. And buttercups and daisies. And thistles...

Sorry! I know it was a long time ago, but I still get homesick when look back.

Most of all, though, I remember the cows. If they hadn't wandered under the old oak tree and done what cows seem to do all the time, there wouldn't have been any Fairy circles. You know, those toadstool rings that grow around the edges of the you-know-what for us to sit on when we had our council meetings.

It was at one of these council meetings that the Elders had the bright idea that I was now old enough to go out into the wide world and fend for myself. And just like committees everywhere, they made a decision.

Now you see, unlike you Humans, Fairies don't have to work to live. Traditionally, our life is one of pleasure and... Well, that's it really.

But when you live for such a very long time, as we do, you get bored out of your tiny mind. Now, doing something, whatever it is, is far better than sitting around doing nothing, and I was willing to try just about anything.

So, it was settled, and I don't mind telling you, what I do is hard work. And it's expensive.

I've got a scale of rates according to the job in hand. The poorer they are, the less I pay. The rich generally benefit most from my services. Yes, I know that sounds a bit unfair, but that's the way it goes.

I've been doing this job now for over a thousand of your years and I shall very probably still be doing it when my wings drop off in a couple of thousand more.

But, if I should *ever* run into that idiot Elder who dreamt up this job for me, he'll find out exactly where I intend to stuff two-and-a-half million tonnes of teeth. ◆

Flight of Fancy

That did it for Howard.

Olive had rubbed his nose in it once too often. Standing there on the edge of the cliff as though she hadn't a care in the world. She had constantly berated Howard about his shortcomings, of which a fear of heights was only one. He'd show her if it was the last thing he ever did.

Suddenly, Olive pointed up at a hang glider soaring high above on a thermal rising from the cliff face.

"See that," she said, shielding her eyes against the mid-afternoon sun. "If you only had the guts..."

Howard remembered how, when he had to go to Paris on business, he had shaken like a leaf all the way to the airport, only to discover that they'd given him a window seat.

That was the moment he found that, being so high up, he wasn't frightened at all.

"All *right.* I'll do it."

It was out before he could stop himself

"You what?" Olive exploded with laughter. "You? Hang-gliding? You'll be the death of me yet."

Tears of derision cascaded down Olive's purple face as she guffawed on, blissfully unaware of the fuse that she had just ignited in Howard's mind, his hatred focusing on that final phrase.

"You'll be the death of me yet!"

The following day, Howard signed up for a course of lessons.

To his great surprise, he took to his enforced hobby with ease. With the sole exception of launching himself from the cliff-top, which he always did with his eyes tight shut, he found the experience totally exhilarating.

As his proficiency improved, he wondered what Olive would say if she knew. She never asked about his ever more frequent absences but, when he was gliding beneath fluffy clouds, his happiness was complete.

Complete, that was... except for Olive.

He thought about leaving her. He could move away from the area and find a nice little cottage somewhere. But that would need money, and everything, even the house, was in Olive's name. The more he thought about it, the more his dreams of heaven became visions of hell.

The problem simmered for weeks and his only release from Olive's rasping tongue was to swoop and soar beneath the clouds at every opportunity.

It had been a very cold day and thermals were difficult to find. He headed along the coast taking lift from up-currents caused by the brisk onshore breeze rising from the cliff face. Beneath him, the ground was an unbroken blanket of white after two days of snow. Distracted by the serenity of the scene, he suddenly felt the nose of the glider drop as he almost stalled.

He swooped to gain speed before an up current took him up again. Then, wheeling high above the cliff he noticed a solitary figure standing at the edge. Even from this distance he was sure it was Olive, her gaze fixed on a ship on the horizon.

"Up here. Why don't you look at me?" he shouted, aware that she couldn't hear him at this distance.

He headed inland for some distance before turning back towards the sea. The clear air gave him a panoramic view of the area.

Despite the cold, with the low winter sun behind him, it felt so good to be free and he dreaded the thought of returning to earth to face Olive's constant bickering.

His rage focused on the tiny figure at the cliff edge and the memory of her laughter, challenging him, taunting him until...

She'd said it herself: "You'll be the death of me."

Two hundred metres... a hundred... fifty...

The figure grew rapidly as he swooped low

over the single line of footprints. He couldn't believe his luck. It would look like suicide.

"Damn you, woman, I hate you," he shrieked as the shadow of his glider fell across her like a giant bird of prey

The figure turned, momentary recognition mingling with terror as she threw herself back to avoid him. Then she was gone, her broken body bouncing from the rock face to rest in a semicircle of red and white foam at the foot of the cliff.

Finally, free of Olive's contempt, Howard turned to get as far from the scene as possible.

Wheeling back towards the cliff, he tried to get lift as the wind dropped momentarily, preventing him from maneuvering close to the cliff face.

He looked down.

This close to the ground, his old fear of heights returned, and he automatically shut his eyes tight. He forced them open but too late to prevent his wingtip making contact, sending him plummeting to join Olive among the rocks below. ♦

The Final Straw

The heavily-laden rope had ceased its steady swing and now hung straight and hard. In the stillness of the early morning there was no breath of wind to cause further movement.

The riderless horse, standing patiently by the tree, turned its head, pricked its ears and snorted. The sounds of the nocturnal desert had faded with the greying of the sky and, slowly at first then faster, the shadows had fled before the approaching day.

The horse, silhouetted against the skyline, had witnessed all this and more. At the distant thunder of hooves, it whinnied softly and pawed the ground once, twice. There was a flutter of white as sunlight caught the note that was tied to the saddle's pommel.

The steady thunder rumbled to a ragged halt and voices drifted on the air. There was a shout. Then an arm pointed towards the tree and the small band rode hurriedly up the rise.

Esteban reached the tree ahead of his men. A knife flashed, the rope parted, and the lifeless body dropped to the ground.

Esteban looked down at the dead man. His white hair and weather-beaten face showed more than age, more than fear, more even than death. Salt crystals that marked the passage of long-dried tears also showed guilt and contrition. That he had prayed for forgiveness could be seen from the rosary beads entwined about the fingers of one hand; fingers that had, in one fateful day, tied the rope and fired the shot...

There was little shade to be found with the sun almost directly overhead. The bell cast a hard shadow against the white floor of the tower of the old adobe mission, providing both protection from the sun and concealment from the crowd. To avoid detection, the old man had waited since before first light, watching the crowd gather in the square.

Now, the young man who addressed the crowd from the dais across the square saw nothing in their eyes to show the feeling in their hearts. Since he had come to power, the peasants were oppressed as never before, such were the taxes and levies he had imposed upon them. A tiny minority had benefited, but the majority had suffered.

Resplendent in military uniform, he paused occasionally for the roar of acclaim that he knew would come. Who would dare deny him his due?

"El Presidente! El Presidente!"

In the tower, the assassin passed a trembling hand across his brow and shifted his position. At the next roar from the crowd, he would be ready.

Beads of perspiration trickled onto the breach of his rifle. He looked down at the trigger guard, around which was knotted the short straw that had condemned him to carry out this dreadful deed.

The moment came.

"El Presidente! El Presidente!"

In an instant it was over. No one heard the shot. To some a god, to most a devil, El Presidente slumped to the ground.

In the silence that fell, unbelieving peasants at first crowded around the body then, as significance dawned, they scattered.

The military leaders knelt beside the body of their puppet and vowed revenge. The assassin must be brought to trial or revolution would reign.

By the time the assassin's hiding place had been discovered, a spent cartridge case was the only sign of his hurried departure. The town was searched, and peasants brutally questioned but none would betray him.

Parties of men were sent in all directions with orders to bring the assassin back for trial. Unwillingly they obeyed, fearful of what would happen to their families should they refuse. They had waited for this day and would answer when the call came but, for now, they must obey.

Such a man was Esteban. He led his men into the desert, silently praying that he would not be the one to bring this man back to face torture and death. It might well have been he who had drawn the short straw.

At first light, they stopped at a fork in the trail to eat a hasty meal. As they did so, one of the men gave a shout and pointed up at the ridge.

Esteban raised his sombrero to shield his eyes from the sun and saw the silhouette on the skyline. The meal forgotten, the group rode hastily up the hill towards the tree.

Looking down at the dead man, Esteban wondered. What kind of man would choose to die rather than live to fight on for the cause? There could be no justification, no forgiveness.

The burial did not take long, just a crude cairn of rocks and a shallow grave scratched out of the poor soil.

Picking up the reins of the dead man's horse and securing them to his saddle. Esteban saw the note. As he read, his eyes softened.

Cutting two small branches from the tree, he fashioned them into a simple cross. Placing it upon the cairn, he hung the old man's rosary upon it, crumpled the note and let it fall between the stones.

In silence, Esteban followed his men down towards the trail. He looked back at the lonely grave then spurred his horse into a canter.

It would be dark soon, but tomorrow's sun would rise on a country in revolution. He was ready. And it was up to him to ensure that the old man's sacrifice would not be in vain.

As they rode, the words he had read ran again through his mind.

"It had to be! In the name of Humanity, it had to be! We drew lots. It was fair. It was fate. No-one else knew that he was my son." ♦

Class Action

Avis wedged open the charity shop door to let in the fresh morning air. Then, pushing aside the plain orange curtain that concealed a tiny kitchen area, she put the kettle on and turned her attention to a large box that someone had left in the doorway.

A number of items were quickly relegated to the rubbish bin. At the bottom of the box were a dozen or so discarded books. Avis wiped them over with a duster and piled them on the counter.

"Good morning, dear. Sorry I'm late."

The breezy greeting came from a tall, prim woman who plonked a loaded shopping bag on the counter and swept up one of the books.

"Oh, wonderful," she crooned, "I've been after this for simply ages. Make the tea will you, Avis dear, I'm absolutely gasping."

Avis busied herself with the kettle.

"Phyllida," she handed a cup to the now-engrossed manageress, "About Peggy..." She tailed off. "What's that you're reading?"

Phyllida looked up.

"Sorry, dear? Oh, this? It's the only one of Meg Carpenter's books I haven't got. I'm her most ardent fan. This came out while I was abroad."

"Look, Phyllida," Avis ignored the other's enthusiasm. "It's about Peggy. I know she has a heart of gold and she does whatever we ask. But, really, you only have to see her to know that she's not... well..."

"Not... one of us?" Phyllida offered.

Avis sighed with relief.

"I'm so glad you understand. I'm not a snob, as you know. Serving ordinary members of the public who come in for a rummage is one thing, but she could put off the people who donate worth-while items to us. Their patronage is so important to our work."

Phyllida smiled.

"I hate to say it but I have the same misgivings. I get an uncanny feeling that she's got something to hide." She paused. "I'm not really sure that I actually trust her..."

"Oh, you don't think...?"

"Oh, no!" Phyllida quickly retracted the implication. "No, dear, of course not. I'm sure she's as honest as the day is long. It's just that... well... she never seems to be very forthcoming. In fact, she doesn't say much at all about... well... about anything."

Avis hesitated. "Perhaps I shouldn't say this but I feel... uneasy when she's around."

Phyllida nodded. "I know exactly what you mean. Yes, perhaps we should find someone to replace her."

"I'd feel a great deal better." Avis made no attempt to stifle a sigh of relief. "And I know someone who might be interested, too. In fact, you already know her... Daphne Morrison?"

"Daphne Morrison? Isn't she the one who writes?"

"That's her. She wanted me to join her circle. Now, she'd fit in beautifully. I'll ask her."

Phyllida finished her tea. "Good idea," she said, handing her cup to Avis and picking up her book again just as Peggy backed into the shop carrying a large box.

"Just a few bits and pieces I thought might sell," she said, putting the box on the counter and pushing her slipping spectacles into place with one finger. "It's surprising what you collect over the years."

Phyllida tried to look enthusiastic, fully expecting to find the box full of what she would call 'tat'. She forced a smile.

"Thank you, dear. I'm sure they'll fetch a welcome few coppers."

She turned and signaled to Avis by looking first at her and then at the street door. Avis responded immediately.

"Oh, Phyllida dear, I wonder if I might just pop out and make a telephone call..."

As the door closed behind her, Phyllida steeled herself for what she had to say to Peggy.

About half an hour passed before Avis returned, accompanied by the elegant Daphne. Avis made coffee and left the two women to become acquainted.

"Of course, I haven't seen you since... oh... Monica Fortnum's divorce party, wasn't it? How is she? Still divorced?" said Phyllida.

Daphne sipped daintily.

"Yes... again. Twice, actually. But... all stripes to her. She did terribly well out of all three."

Phyllida raised her eyebrows. "Well! Well done her!"

"I understand from Avis that you're looking for someone to start right away." Said Daphne, changing the subject.

Suddenly, Avis gasped and held up a figurine.

"Look at these items that Peggy left. This is Meissen." She delved among the paper wrappings. "Here's another... and this is Dresden. We were right after all. We'd better call the police."

"I knew it!" said Phyllida. "When she came in this morning, she told me she was moving so I didn't actually have to dismiss her. She apologised for the short notice but she didn't say where she was moving to... just that she was in a hurry."

"I'm not surprised." Avis held up yet another trinket. "It's obvious from all this stuff that she must be on the run..."

"Good Lord," said Daphne, suddenly rummaging in her handbag. "I had no idea that it could be so exciting working here. What an absolutely super plot for a novel."

Daphne produced a notebook out of her handbag and clicked a ball-pen into life.

Phyllida picked up the box.

"We'd better put these away safely. They could be needed as evidence. I just knew that she was hiding something."

She had only just concealed the box in the kitchen when Peggy walked in. She reached down beside the counter and picked up a carrier bag.

"Sorry," she said. "Forgot my shopping."

Suddenly her face lit up.

"Oh, hello, Daphne. How are you?"

Avis and Phyllida stared, speechless.

"Well, hello, yourself," said Daphne, starting to rise, but Peggy was already heading towards the door.

"Sorry. Must dash," she said brightly. "Moving house. You know how it is. Lovely to see you again. Keep up the good work."

The door clattered shut behind her.

"But... that's her," blurted Avis, springing into perplexed motion. "The absolute gall of the woman. We must call the police."

"No. Just a moment," Phyllida recovered her voice. "Daphne, you know her. You must know where she lives?"

"Peggy Wood?" Daphne shrugged. "Oh, I don't actually know her. We met at the Circle."

"But she seemed to know you well enough. What did she mean by keeping up the good work?"

"Oh, that! Something and nothing really. She was a great help to me when I was starting out with my first novel." Daphne looked wistful. "Actually, I'm still working on it, but I didn't like to say. She really is the most helpful of mentors. To be honest, I'm surprised you didn't recognise her. I know she wears glasses now but that's her photo on the back of the book you're reading. She writes under the name of Meg Carpenter." ♦

Flight to Chefick

"But there's no such place as Dolgrage!"

Of course, the stewardess was right, and Alvin Grant knew it.

Things had been... well... a little confused ever since the Arrivals board had thrown a fit earlier on.

"Where is he now?" he wanted to know.

For a moment, the stewardess looked about to lose her cool. She pointed towards the VIP lounges. Grant headed off in that direction.

As he entered the lounge, a small, chunky figure rose to meet him.

"My friends? They have arrived?"

The voice had a strange, chanting quality that defied recognition.

Grant left the question suspended and accepted the outstretched hand, despite the fluorescent green of the man's skin.

"I'm sorry to keep you waiting, Mr... er?"

"Xreetle. Klyn Xreetle."

"Sreetle?" Grant tried the name on for size. "Forgive me, sir. I find the pronunciation a little unusual..."

The other dismissed the detail with a wave.

Doubting, now, that the man was a fraud, Grant asked if it was correct that he had just arrived from Dolgrage.

There was a green nod of confirmation.

"Flight number FRXD 7. And I am waiting only to meet my colleagues and to learn of the departure time of our flight to Chefick this afternoon."

"To where, sir?"

An eerie feeling started to gather at the back of Grant's neck.

"To Chefick..."

Grant was finding it difficult not to look as skeptical as he felt.

"Forgive me but... er... may I ask, where... exactly... is Chefick? Geography was never my subject."

"Ah, yes!" Xreetle looked thoughtful. "How best to say?"

"Got him!"

Grant was elated. So, it was a put-up job, after all. His elation faded as the little man spread out on the table a fairly detailed map of the world.

Well... sort of.

"Latitude 96 degrees North, Longitude 292 degrees West. There is Chefick."

A green finger indicated a totally unfamiliar land-mass.

Grant's blood pressure shot up like a nudist in a nettle bed. This could drive a man to drink. The idea appealed to him.

He mumbled something about checking up on flight times and headed for his favourite bar.

Within minutes, a soothing alcoholic fog had descended, calming his shattered nerves as he unloaded his confusion on the barman.

"He had a map with a full three-hun'ert 'n' sixty degrees of longitude, east and west, an' a hun'ert 'n' eighty degrees of latitude, north 'n' south. That's more degrees than there are in the whole world, Sham."

Sam listened with an experienced ear. He breathed unhygienically on glasses, polished them and hung them on the overhead rack.

"Now look, Mr Grant," he said in a kindly tone as soon as Grant had slithered to a halt. "We've known each other for what... ten years? Twelve, maybe? But... little green men? You must've been on some bender..."

"Who else would listen. Sham? The Old Man'd pro'bly fire me jus' for the hell of it. But there's a green guy in Room 801 who's waiting for a flight that doesn't exist to a place that doesn't exist either."

He reached across the bar and placed a conspiratorial hand on Sam's shoulder.

"Sham, do me a favour an' take him a drink with my compliments. Then come and tell me I'm not crazy."

The barman returned, looking even more puzzled.

"Sorry, Mr Grant. He's there, all right.

Queer little cove, ain't he. Where'd you say he comes from?"

"Dolgrage. But that's just a name that came up on the Arrivals board this morning. There were lots of strange place names like... well... er... Ygington... Ninoa... Tiva... Chefick.... That sort of..."

Grant's jaw dropped, and his eyes widened. "Chefick!"

He was suddenly sober.

"Sam, I've got it. That's where he said he was flying on to..."

It was warm in the computer room. Grant listened intently as the engineer pointed to a charred component on a small printed-circuit board and explained how it had affected the Arrivals board that morning.

"There are hundreds of identical boards inside the computer. They're all individually numbered. So, if something goes wrong, all we have to do is to locate the circuit that's gone on the blink, whip it out and plug another one in."

If Grant had been asked whether he had understood the explanation, the words 'clear as mud' would probably have escaped his lips.

"Could the same thing happen to the Departures board as well?"

"Absolutely! If the same board had burnt

out."

The engineer opened panels on both computers.

"See? They're identical."

Grant thanked him and left.

An hour later Grant climbed back onto the bar stool.

"It's all right now, Sam," he said, confidently. "It's solved."

"It ain't, you know." Sam poured Grant's favourite tipple. "You've missed all the fun. About half an hour ago, the Departure board did the same as the Arrivals one did this morning. The same funny names came up again and no-one knew what was happening. The Old Man was running around swearing he'd have someone's guts for garters."

"No, he won't," Grant grinned. "I told him it was down to me."

Sam's eyebrows shot up. "So, when do you leave?"

"I don't." Grant leaned across the bar and dropped his voice. "I waited until the engineer went to lunch Then I slipped into the computer room and swapped the dud board from the Arrivals computer for the good one with the same number in the Departures computer. That's why those strange names came up again. Then I told that green chap that his flight to Chefick was waiting."

"I still don't get it." Sam looked puzzled.

"The Old Man didn't believe it, either. When I told him about the green chap, he told me I was crazy, so I went out to the plane with him so that he could see for himself. Now, we had a passenger on a flight that didn't exist to a place that didn't exist, so it stands to reason that he didn't exist either. Right? But we both saw him."

Sam's expression was a picture.

"The Old Man was so keen to prove that I'd slipped a cog that he actually boarded the plane to see this chap for himself, I was careful not to follow, and it was just then that the computer was put right again."

He tossed back the rest of his drink in one gulp.

"You know. Sam, I don't think we'll be seeing the Old Man again for a while. Well, at least, not until the next flight comes in from Chefick!" ♦

Fly Away, Peter

"Madeleine?"

The voice at the other end of the phone was high-pitched with excitement.

"Madeleine, did you hear what I said? They've found Peter's plane. They've just shown it on the television."

The phone almost slipped from Madeleine's arthritic grasp as she sank slowly onto the settee to take in the news.

She let the handset rest in her lap, oblivious to the concern in her sister's thin, insect-like voice that called to her from it.

Several moments passed before she replaced it to her ear.

"Sorry, dear," she said distantly. "But are you sure? I mean, have they actually *said* that it was his?"

"Well, I had a call from a chap called Allington. He was in Peter's squadron. He said they were certain that it is Peter's plane. There weren't that many Hurricanes went down in that area of the Fens. He rang my number because yours is unlisted. Apparently, he joined Peter's squadron just a few weeks before..."

Sally's voice tailed off.

"Before Peter went missing."

Madeleine finished her sister's sentence.

"It's all right, dear. After all these years, I have got used to the idea that he isn't coming back."

Her words must have sounded a little blasé, she thought, and felt her chin begin to tremble as tears moistened the corners of her eyes.

"Are you all right? You don't sound it."

Sally's concern returned.

"Mustn't give way," Madeleine thought. Then, to Sally: "Yes. I'm fine, dear. Thank you for letting me know. I'll talk to you later."

She was about to hang up when she realized that Sally was still speaking.

"Sorry, dear, what was that?"

"He wants to come and talk to you, so I've arranged for him to come round later this afternoon. He should be there at about three o'clock. I'll be back by then."

Tears began to trace the lines of age down Madeleine's face. She hung up with an almost imperceptible "Goodbye" and let the tears come.

The memory of Peter's cheery smile on that summer morning had never dimmed. Even more than half a century later it was as though he had never left her. Certainly, he had never left her thoughts. The moment she awoke and when she finally switched out the light, he was there. That she rarely dreamed and, worse, that she never remembered dreaming of Peter had sometimes caused her to wonder if her waking memories had simply become a habit. But that spark, that thrill that comes with a lover's touch, had always accompanied the memories.

"Don't worry," he had said when the telegram arrived recalling him to his squadron. "The sooner we beat them, the sooner we can be together."

Madeleine was not convinced that his apparent disregard for danger was genuine, but her heart would not let her believe otherwise. His corn-gold hair fell forward, touching her lightly on the forehead and mingling with her own as he leant down to kiss her. Then he had vanished into the steam and the subdued excitement of the crowded platform.

Her hand automatically reached out as though to grasp the last vestige of him as he disappeared, and the words of the old children's rhyme tumbled from her lips with all the fervency of a prayer.

"Come back, Peter."

The train began to move. Madeleine almost ran from the station. Of course he would come back.

She looked at the wedding ring that Peter had placed on her finger scarcely an hour before. There could never be anyone else.

Hadn't they planned in the few short months of their engagement that, when it was over, they'd settle down in a small cottage near Tunbridge Wells. They'd raise three children, they'd have a dog and two cats and a pony for the children. And the rest of the world could do what it liked. It would all be so wonderful, so perfect.

Sally had always treated Peter like a brother and was wonderfully supportive when the telegram had arrived.

But Madeleine was not blind to the obvious anguish behind Sally's help and encouragement and her grief was muted by the worldly veneer that protected her from the attentions of her many potential suitors.

"There's a letter here from Essex?" Sally had said, dropping it onto the breakfast table.

It was postmarked exactly as Peter's letters had been and, when Sally began to clear the table a few minutes later Madeleine was still staring at it.

"Aren't you going to open it?"

Sally picked up the letter. She was about to place it on the mantle-piece next to a photograph of Peter standing beside his plane when she hesitated and said, matter-of-factly, "Well, if you won't open it, then, I will."

Before Madeleine could stop her. Sally had

opened the envelope to reveal several sheets of hand-written paper folded around a sealed envelope addressed to Madeleine in Peter's handwriting.

Sally scanned the letter and let it drop onto the table. Then, without a word, she left the room and, as the door closed, Madeleine picked up the letter.

"Dear Mrs Cranshaw," it began, "I'm sure that by now you will have received official notification that your husband, Flight Lieutenant Peter Cranshaw, has been listed as missing in action..."

It went on to explain that Peter had not returned from a reconnaissance mission over Holland. His Hurricane was last seen trailing smoke over the North Sea. He could have bailed out but he seemed to regain control and apparently had sufficient height to make it back to base.

He had not arrived. This was typical of his courage and conduct in the service of his country.

The letter was signed by Peter's commanding officer.

Madeleine turned Peter's letter over and held it to her lips.

Her jumbled thoughts pleaded with her to open it; to read of his love so that she could carry it with her forever. At the same time, they told her not to open it; that she knew what it said – what it must say – and to carry that in her heart until he returned and there would be no need for words.

She remembered her own words at the station.

"Come back, Peter."

Then she had gone to her bedroom and taken a chocolate box from a drawer, carefully placed the letter, unopened, on top of the others and closed the drawer. She curled up on the bed and lay staring into space as the first tear fell onto the pillow, followed by another and another in ever increasing numbers until sleep came.

"It all happened a very long time ago, Mr Allington,"

Madeleine studied the old man's face as she handed him a cup of tea. "I'm most grateful to you for coming all this way."

"Peter loved you very much, Mrs Cranshaw. There was never any doubt. I don't know whether you're aware of the sort of conversation that goes on in the Officers' Mess in wartime. But, while the chaps might talk about their latest conquest, they rarely talked about their truly loved ones. It was as though doing so might. in some way, expose them to some danger or other. Peter was as protective of you as anyone I'd ever met."

"Thank you," Madeleine smiled, looking almost coy. "I would expect nothing less of him. He was the most perfect of gentlemen." For a moment, the years seemed to drop away. "But then, I would think that, wouldn't I? That's what made it all so wonderful. Of course, there could never have been—has never been—anyone else."

The old man smiled. "Even after all these years. I hope he was aware of what he had. I'm sure that he was. No. I'm certain of it, Mrs Cranshaw. He never took off without your picture in the pocket of his flying jacket."

His tone took on a more serious note and he sat forward in his chair.

"Mrs Cranshaw, when we raised Peter's plane from the marsh it was in fairly good condition. Preserved by the mud so to speak. I don't wish to distress you, so please forgive me if I don't go into too much detail. Suffice to say that... Peter... was still inside. There will, of course, be a proper funeral with full military honours in the not too distant future..."

He broke off as Madeleine got up without a word and took down Peter's picture from the mantelpiece.

"Oh, I'm sorry."

He rose to help her back to her chair.

"I'm sorry. I've upset you. Perhaps I should

come back another time..."

"Oh no. Mr Allington. You haven't upset me at all. You see, I have my memories. I said my goodbyes to Peter a long time ago. I just needed to see his face while we talked."

"Yes, of course. I understand." Mr Allington produced a manila envelope from his pocket. "There is never a good time I know, but I think this might be as good a time as any to give you this. It was still in his pocket when we found him. It's a little the worse for wear but still recognisable. I'm sure he would have wanted you to have it."

Madeleine took the envelope and held it gently to her lips. She turned silently towards the open French window and looked out cross the lawn.

"My sister Sally will be here shortly," Madeleine paused. "She was hoping to be back before you arrived. I'm sure she'd like to hear what you have to say. But, if you wouldn't mind, I'd like a few moments alone..."

When Sally arrived, Mr Allington was standing by the French doors, looking out at the small figure sitting in the shade of a tree. A thistledown, caught in the lace of Madeleine's cuff, fluttered casually in the light breeze.

She made no move to brush it away.

Mr Allington did not look round.

"I'm so sorry," he said. "I think she was happy at the end."

Sally joined him at the window.

"What's that she's holding?"

"It's the picture that Peter took with him on every mission. She wanted a few moments alone. Perhaps to see it again and remember. But I'm afraid she never even opened the envelope."

Sally said nothing.

"She was very beautiful as a young woman. So very elegant with all that long dark hair," the old man continued, "Having seen the photo, I can understand why Peter loved her so much. And to think that she held on to that love all these years. How very sad that it ended as it did. Fate can be so cruel."

Sally turned and picked up a framed photograph and handed it to him. It was of two fair-haired sisters playing together.

"Perhaps not," she said. ♦

The Hunted

"You're not serious?" Hob's expression was incredulous.

"Now look'ee here, son,"

The mayor was using the patronising tone he usually kept for the run-up to election day.

"I don't have to tell you this here's a small community an' there ain't that many of us had the benefit of a university ed'cation. An' I don't..."

"No, Mayor Gurney, you *don*'t have to remind me."

Hob had heard it all before and, this time, he was ready.

"And you don't have to lie to me any more, either."

He watched the mayor's expression change before continuing.

"There's no need to look so surprised. I was bound to find out one day. My ma kept the secret just like you made her promise—right up to the day she died. But she couldn't go to meet her Maker with it on her conscience. She sent me to fetch a priest and I overheard her confession."

The mayor flushed with embarrassment and started to huff.

"Wh... why, that's all in the past now, son. An' there weren't nothin' I could do to stop it.

Nobody paid no never mind to me. I was jus' a young deputy doin' my job... and there was too many o' them, anyways."

Hob tried to stop the mayor floundering in guilty recollection.

"You had a gun. You could have done something."

"What could I have done? If I'd started shootin' there'd have been two of us dead, maybe more, 'stead of just the one. They bust into that jailhouse an' locked me in a cell. Then they drug your paw out and strung him up. I tell you, boy, there weren't nothin' I could do."

The mayor's indignation suddenly turned to full-blooded anger.

"An' besides, this here happened more'n thirty years ago. You wasn't but a tick an' still in diapers. I know he was your paw an' all, but you was too young to know him. But we did our darndest to set matters to rights. We kep' it from you for your own good. Did our best for your maw, too. Helped her to bring you up and put you through law school. Well, there ain't but a few of us old timers left now an' most of the townsfolk don't even know what took place back then. I sure as hell ain't gonna tell 'em. An' I'm damned sure this ain't the time for you to enlighten 'em, neither. Right now the whole town is scared. They needs your help. Y'owes them that at least. Then you can do what the hell you like."

"For Crissakes, Mayor Gurney,"

Hob banged the table with his fist and glared at the old man.

"They hanged my daddy 'cos they said he was a werewolf. Now, you think there's another on the loose an' you want me to help fight it? You must be out of your goddamn mind!"

Hob rubbed his eyes and looked up at the library clock. Almost four-thirty. He wriggled his shoulders to banish the stiffness that had started to set in more than an hour ago. His chair scraped on the floor as he pushed it back and stood up. The sound echoed about the walls of the vaulted room.

Returning the pile of books that had accumulated on the table to their respective shelves took him through metaphysics and mythology to fable and superstition and a variety of other abstruse subjects.

Finishing the task just as the bell rang to warn visitors that the library would be closing in fifteen minutes, he stuffed a pile of photocopies into his briefcase and walked thoughtfully out into the late autumn dusk.

Despite the thickness of Hob's overcoat, the chill wind bit deep. His gloved fingers were soon numb, and the briefcase became steadily heavier as he headed for his hotel.

The wound in the calf of his left leg ached. Probably all that sitting down over the past two weeks, he thought, ignoring a flashing 'Don't Walk' sign and the expletives hurled at him by swerving cab drivers.

In his room, Hob pored over the pile of information collected from the library. There was no way that the township of Henshaw could attribute the mysterious rise of wolf attacks to the supernatural.

Werewolves had been part of mythology for centuries. Reports of such attacks over the years could, at best, be attributed to superstitions brought over by the vast influx of early European immigrants.

Hob sat back, satisfied that he'd concluded his mission. He could return to Henshaw and set the townsfolk's minds to rest.

When the attacks had started, evidence had pointed to the possibility of a cougar foraging to feed its young. Cattle had been found with their throats torn open. At first, just the odd one here and there, then more. Perhaps eight months had passed before any human had fallen victim. Then they had found Nathan Rush.

His injuries seemed far greater than a normal wolf could have inflicted. Rumours had persisted, however, that this wolf walked on two legs by day and stalked its prey by the light of the full moon.

The powers of the werewolf were, after all, supernatural. Like those of the vampire, they were widely documented and, to Hob's legal mind, as much at variance with each other as they were with common sense.

Somewhere in the distance, a clock chimed one. Hob yawned and got up to let the cold night air in to clear his head. He looked out across the city at frost-covered buildings sparkling under a waxing moon. Suddenly, his leg was aching badly, and he prepared for bed, dreading tomorrow's task of presenting his findings to a disbelieving Mayor Gurney.

Sleep was elusive. Vivid recollections of nights spent hunting for the wolf trampled through Hob's exhausted mind. The pain in his leg was now almost unbearable. He tried to sleep, only to be woken time and again by memories of the wolf leaping out of the night. Its jaws, anchored deep in the flesh of the calf just below his knee, had dragged him from his terrified horse. Only a bullet from his still-holstered revolver had saved Hob from further injury.

By morning, the pain had dulled, and Hob was on his way back to Henshaw, determined to make the townsfolk see sense.

"Ain't nothin' happened while you been gone, son"

The mayor wasted no time on formalities as Hob climbed down from the train.

"I guess we can fergit all that namby-pamby nonsense 'bout werewolves an' all. But I sure as hell want to thank you for humourin' a stupid old man."

Hob sighed with frustration and said nothing. Two whole weeks wasted.

Two nights later a wolf howled close to the edge of town. Within minutes, the whole town was saddling up for yet another night hunt.

Hob led a small party out in the bright moonlight. Eerie shadows patterned the landscape, beating past beneath thrashing hooves. In the distance, a darker shadow moved into a stand of trees at the crest of a rise. Hob ordered his party to surround the trees in case the wolf made a break for the other side.

As they converged on the trees and the darkness engulfed them, Hob was aware of sudden movement. His horse screamed and reared as something monstrous and grey exploded out of the shadows straight at him, bringing the horse down, hurling Hob to the ground as blackness enveloped him.

When his senses returned, Hob was lying on a bunk in the tiny Henshaw jailhouse. His right shoulder was tightly bandaged and throbbed painfully. His head hurt and the pain in his leg had returned. Outside, he could hear voices raised in anger.

As his eyes opened, Doc Solomon was about to administer an injection.

"Just hold it there, Doc. Looks like he's a'comin' round."

Mayor Gurney's voice came from beyond Hob's line of vision.

"Let's see what he has to say fer hisself."

"What happened?" Hob asked weakly.

"That's just what we was hopin' you'd tell us, boy."

Hob tried to remember but it had all happened too quickly; a rush of movement, screams of terror, first horses then men. Horrible gurglings like strangled pleas for help, for mercy. Then darkness. It made no sense.

"I don't remember. There were others. Ask them."

"Wish we could, boy."

The Mayor's face came into view over the top of Hob's head. He puffed cigar smoke into Hob's upturned eyes, making him blink and cough. "They's all dead. Ever' last one of them."

Chewing his cigar from one side of his mouth to the other, he took it out and focused on the butt.

"But, I guess you wouldn't know 'bout that, neither."

Hob struggled to sit up, but his ankle was handcuffed to the bunk.

"What's this? Am I under arrest or something?"

"More than that, boy. You'se in custody for your own pertection."

"Protection? From what?"

The mayor nipped the end off a new cigar as more angry voices rose outside the barred window.

"From the good townsfolk o' Henshaw, boy. They wants to string you up, just like they did your dear ol' daddy when you was a little bitty kid. Only, this time, I ain't even gonna try and stop 'em. There was killings then, too. In them days, we didn't need no scientific proof. Ever'one know'd he killed them. First animals, then people. T'weren't no ornery wolf, neither. We all know'd that."

"But that's just superstition."

"The killings stopped, didn't they? This time, they'll stop for keeps. *You* ain't got no kids."

As the two men left, leaving the cell door open, the Mayor turned.

"Oh! An' so you won't go to your maker wonderin' how come we know'd it was you, I'll tell you. When we heard the ruckus, we see a wolf—bigger'n any I ever seen—tearing at ever'thin' in sight. Several of us shot at it and we seen it hit in the right shoulder. Then the moon clouded over and we lost it. When we could see again, there weren't no sign of any wolf, jus' you with a bullet in your right shoulder. Well, we all reckon that there's proof aplenty."

He opened the door. The jail instantly filled with people—some fearful, some cursing, some praying.

Hob was bundled unceremoniously outside by countless eager hands. A rope was thrown over a beam and one end was quickly fashioned into a noose.

The crowd fell silent as Hob was hauled onto a pick-up truck and the noose was placed over his head.

"You got anythin' to say, boy?"

The Mayor parted the crowd and stepped forward.

Hob struggled to find words that would convince them of their mistake.

"What proof do you have? Why don't you keep me locked up? Then, when the next killing happens, you'll know it couldn't have been me. Hang me and you'll live with it for the rest of your lives."

Mayor Gurney slapped the side of the truck to signal the driver to start the engine.

"There wasn't no killin's while you was

away, boy. They started again when you come back..."

Suddenly, the hubbub was silenced by a frantic horn blaring out at the far end of the street, and the crowd scattered as another pickup truck slid to a halt and the driver scrambled out.

'Didn't think I was goin' to make it," he gasped.

He let down the tailgate and threw back a tarpaulin.

"I found this down to the crick."

He dragged out a large grey carcass, matted with blood from a gaping bullet wound in its right shoulder. It hit the road with a slap.

Mayor Gurney chewed on his cigar and spat.

"Well, if that ain't the biggest darned wolf I ever did see..."

A wave of surprise and relief ran through the crowd.

Eager hands quickly removed the noose from Hob's neck and set him down on the ground.

Ignoring embarrassed apologies, Hob made his way home and waited for the day to end.

Suddenly aware that the pain in his leg was gone, he rolled up his jeans to find that the wound had healed while he had been unconscious.

That must have been when the wolf had died. He had survived its attack and now, if there was any truth in those old legends, he would inherit its appetites.

As the full moon rose above the horizon, Hob felt the first stirrings of an unquenchable thirst.

He ran his long tongue around lupine jaws and howled.

Tonight, there would be blood. ♦

<u>Spirit Level</u>

Miss Goodbody knew what was keeping Harry.

There was no point denying it, his drinking had been beyond a joke for months. This time, she would have to face it. If he missed the start of the séance it would be the end of everything.

He was perfectly well aware what was expected of him.

Wasn't it he who had suggested to her in the first place that a few special effects would be good for business? The punters—she wished he wouldn't use these crude expressions—the *clients* had a right to expect something in return for their hard-earned cash. Reluctantly, though, she had to admit that he'd been right.

Not that Miss Goodbody ever actually charged for her services. But she couldn't really begrudge Harry his 'wee dram', and there was no doubt that a few convincing manifestations had helped his cup to run over.

Whatever problems she had experienced in the past with Harry's drinking, she could not deny that he *always* did his homework. But, the last time she had found it necessary to raise the subject, he had threatened to share her secret with the world at large.

Miss Goodbody switched on a small lamp and drew the heavy plush curtains just as the old grandfather clock chimed quarter-to-nine. The clients would be arriving at any moment.

Breathing a sigh of relief, she heard the back-door slam, followed by the unmistakable sounds of Harry muttering drunkenly to himself in the adjoining room.

A knock at the front door prevented her from telling Harry what she thought of his behaviour. Vowing to talk to him later, she gave the room a quick squirt of air freshener to cover the smell of whisky that she knew would soon find its way under the communicating door.

As the visitors filed in and seated themselves around the circular table, a tall elderly man introduced himself as representing a well-known society that had been responsible for the unmasking of many bogus mediums.

"And so I hope you won't mind if I sit in and study your *modus operandi*, so to speak," he concluded.

"Not at all Mr... er...?" Miss Goodbody hid her true feelings by pretending to forget his name.

"Struther. Major Struther!"

She switched off the light and joined her guests at the table.

"Very well, Major. Ladies and gentlemen. Shall we begin?"

She had long ago considered the manner in which to face this moment.

"Let us all hold hands."

The final act had begun.

Miss Goodbody closed her eyes and drew in a deep breath, held it for an expressive moment, then let it slowly escape with a hiss. Minutes passed, during which her face became blank and drawn, and her heavy, even breathing faded into the familiar trance.

"Is there anybody there?' she intoned in an impressive *sotto voce*.

"Aye. There is that."

It was all Miss Goodbody could do not to give the game away herself as Harry's voice boomed out. She had been expecting the usual soft tones of her 'Indian' guide, Chief Thunderclap. Harry was obviously too drunk to remember such piffling details.

"Have you any messages for those assembled here?" she monotoned.

"Aye, I have that."

Despite the air freshener, the smell of whisky was beginning to notice.

"That's quite a group you've got there the night, hen. You can tell the mon on your left that he's a fool. So's anybody who backs Rangers to lose at home."

Miss Goodbody heard a movement from the direction of Major Struther. Probably turning up his concealed tape recorder. She could almost feel his excitement at the idea of exposing this phoney set-up.

"And you can tell the auld biddy with the flowers on her hat that she's wasting her time," Harry went on. "Her dear departed husband does'nae want to hear her nagging tongue again. It was difficult enough to get awa' from it when he was alive, so can she no' let him rest now he's deed."

Harry's victim gasped but said nothing. A young couple sitting across the table from her sniggered. They glanced at each other briefly.

"Aye, and you can hald yer whist." Harry turned his attention to the young girl. "Did you think yon weddin' ring makes everything all right? You should hear what you neighbours have tae say aboot that. They're a canny lot. You've never fooled them for a moment."

The girl's embarrassed squeal was more than Miss Goodbody was prepared to take. Her fake trance was gone in a flash. The damage had already been done.

"That's quite enough, Harry," she snapped, then stood up, about to dismiss the gathering with a profuse, albeit pointless, apology.

"Aw, sit down, y'auld fool. Can ye no see that you've nothing to fear frae these folks. There's not one o' them that's what they seem. They're just here for the show. They don't believe that you can talk with the dead."

"Well, really, Miss Goodbody," Major Struther harrumphed. "I had heard that you and your accomplice were extremely convincing. That is. of course, why I attended this... this... farce. I made my interest perfectly clear at the outset. I have exposed dozens of fakes in the past, but I must say that they did at least try to emulate some level of authenticity"

"Emulate some level of authenticity?" Harry echoed derisively. "Aw, quit your blethering, mon. I doubt if you even know what it means. You came here to expose a fraud. Och, let's start wi' yersel, *Sergeant-*Major Struther. It's surprisin' what you can find out on the spirit level."

The rudely demoted man bristled with anger.

"Well, really! This has gone quite far enough." He shot to his feet. "I have never been so insulted. Miss Goodbody—if that is indeed your real name. You are an unmitigated fraud. When my society hears what has taken place here tonight, steps will be taken—legal steps—to put you where you rightly belong."

Harry's voice boomed out again.

"Aye! You'd know all about that, would you

no', *Sergeant-Major.* If yon Court of Enquiry knew what really happened to the mess funds, would you be here the noo? Would you no' be where *you* rightly belong?"

There was a loud knock at the front door.

"That'll be the bobbies, I should'nae wonder."

A few moments later Miss Goodbody ushered a burly police sergeant into the room. She went to the window and drew back the curtains.

"Very well, Major." She turned to face her accuser. "Perhaps you'd like the sergeant, here, to help you search for hidden loudspeakers."

A hearty chuckle welled up from behind an armchair. Major Struther pulled the chair away from the wall. There was no loudspeaker. He turned his attention to other potential hiding places, finally throwing open the door to the adjoining room. It was empty.

"But... but... this woman is a fraud and a cheat, officer." He turned to the sergeant. "I insist that you arrest her this instant."

Miss Goodbody picked up a vase from the sideboard that stood in front of the window. She looked very small and frail. Then, as though her strength had suddenly returned, she smiled at Major Struther.

"You're right. I *am* a fraud. But not a cheat. I met Harry McWhorter at a séance just like this. We've been together ever since. A good man, in spite of his taste for whisky. Now, how may I help you, sergeant?"

The sergeant looked around at the expectant faces.

"It appears that while Mr McWhorter was under the influence of alcohol, he drove his van into the river."

"Serves him damn well right, if you ask me," interrupted Struther.

"He'd been dead for some time when we got there."

Disbelieving glances passed between the others.

The young woman squealed nervously and hid her face in her hands. Harry chuckled again. The smell of whisky grew heavier—then vanished.

"Are you ready then, hen?"

"Coming Harry, dear."

Handing the vase to the now-speechless Major Struther. Miss Goodbody crossed to the door and was gone.

The Major looked down at the vase. His hand trembled, and a small trickle of dust drifted down the front of his impeccable navy-blue trousers as he read the inscription engraved on the lid.

'Ermintrude Goodbody, 1842-1902'♦

The Last of Lorna

The line of cars stopped at the cemetery gate to allow the funeral director to take his place at the front of the cortege and lead the coffin to its final resting place on foot. Ryan waited until the hearse was alongside and fell into step.

The cortege stopped at the grassy path that led to the open grave. The pall bearers alighted and, solemnly sliding the coffin onto their shoulders, set off along the path with measured tread.

Ryan had always hated funerals. He would not have attended this one if there had been any other choice. He ran his eye along the row of private cars, surprised that there were more than he had expected.

"I am the Resurrection and the Life..."

As the priest droned on, Ryan looked around. Something irritated him as he watched the coffin being lowered into the ground. After a short while, he realised that it was the tears. Or, rather, the lack of them.

He would not have expected Barney or Travis to show grief. In fact, he was surprised to see them here at all.

They had all loved Lorna, but that was in the past. That apart, Ryan was glad to see them. Only one of the old crowd was missing, he thought, but then JJ was sure to be here later.

As the mourners made their way back to the waiting cars, Ryan and the rest of the old gang drifted into a group around the still-open grave and looked down into it.

"Hey there, guys. How you been keeping?" JJ appeared from nowhere. "Funerals are boring, ain't they just? Still, great to see you guys again. Been a long time."

Ryan looked round the circle of faces.

"I guess I was to blame for the way we split up, but I couldn't take it any longer. And I'd do the same again like a shot, so I'm not apologising."

JJ held up a commanding hand.

"Hey, we'd have done the same. Right, guys?"

The others nodded.

JJ laughed. "Well, it's water under the bridge now. Things can be just the way they used to be now that Lorna's... er... no longer available?"

"It won't be nearly the same without Elliot," said Barney.

"Yeah," said Ryan. "Elliot's a great guy. He saved my life in Nam. I can never forget that. He was the only guy in the gang who wasn't cheating with Lorna behind my back.

Everything was rosy till I found out and sent each of you on your way. How long has it been?”

“Nine years,” grunted Barney.

“Four and a half,” said Travis.

“Ten days,” said JJ.

Ryan pulled himself to his full height.

“OK. Now, we put it behind us. Right?

There was a chorus of agreement.

Barney stared down into the grave.

“OK. But I think you should know... You had it wrong about us. You broke up the gang because you were so all-fired sure we were all cheating with her. Actually, it was only Elliot. I guess everybody knew but you.”

Ryan looked puzzled. “How’s that?”

“We knew how you felt about her,” said Travis

JJ shrugged. “He saved your life. Would you have believed us?”

Ryan frowned. “So, you all paid the price instead?”

“Hell, you were married to her. It wasn’t down to us to tell you,” said Barney. “Better you didn’t know. It’s too late to put matters right now.”

Ryan shrugged. “Maybe not. What if Elliot... er... joined us?”

Four arms reached out and linked hands over the fresh grave.

Elliot was the last of the mourners to leave the reception. He let his car roll some way down the hill towards the town before firing up the engine.

Approaching the sweeping curve above the creek, he touched the brake. Suddenly, there were four figures in his path. As he swung the wheel hard over, the door burst open, hurling his passenger out onto the road. Suddenly destabilised by the change of load, the car slid over the edge.

The four figures watched as the white circle of foam spread and drifted lazily downstream, then turned to where Elliot was crouching over, trying to revive the crumpled form on the other side of the road.

"Hey, you OK?"

"She'll be fine," said Ryan.

Elliot stared up at the voice.

"But... but..." he spluttered, pointing to Ryan, "The funeral...?"

Ryan waved him to silence.

"The door of JJ's car jammed, and I went over with him. I guess I was wrong about all of you. No matter. The gang's back together now."

The girl moved. Slowly picking herself up, she looked around at the empty road then over the edge at the dark water. Trembling, her face wet with tears, she started unsteadily down the hill towards the town.

"She'll survive," said Ryan. "She'll find another sucker to snuggle up to. We're all better off without her."

He looked around at the others.

"Well, I guess we've seen the last of Lorna. Time to go."

The five friends reached out and their right hands touched.

In the evening light, they faded and were gone. ◆

Girl Talk

Angela! Darling!

So lovely to see you again. It must be so wonderful actually living in the West End.

Do forgive me for dropping in like this. Of course, I had no idea that you were going out to dinner.

I won't keep you long, but I'm simply bursting to talk to someone and, as I was passing, I thought...

Well, hel-lo! So this is the Aidan I've heard so much about?

Hello, Aiden, I'm Stella, one of Angela's old school chums.

Well... not that old, actually.

Ooh, such a strong manly grip. Mmm! I'll bet he's a real dark horse. O-oh, yes!

But you will excuse us for a few moments, won't you Aiden, sweetie. You won't mind, will you?

You know... girl talk? Just for a few moments? Oh, Thank you so much. I knew you'd understand...

Now, Angela, darling, as I was saying...

I simply had to tell someone about the fantastic adventure I had while I was shopping this afternoon.

It really began this morning when I decided, right out of the blue, that I was desperately in need of some retail therapy. I came up on the 9.42 from Tunbridge Wells and went straight into a coffee bar just off Trafalgar Square. Dreadful coffee but the loos are so much better than those at the station. And free!

Well, I spent the rest of the morning imagining what I'd like to buy. I had a snack and then spent most of the afternoon in the Bond Street area where, eventually—of course—I ended up in Mayberry's.

Well, as usual, I started at the 'if-only' end and I had my eye on an elegantly-tailored suit about half way towards the 'as-long-as-I-don't-eat-for-a-month' end, when a slender arm, with long delicate fingers, an expensive French manicure and a massive Rolex wristwatch came through the rack and took it from right under my nose.

I parted the other items on the rack and found myself face to face with the most elegant of women. She smiled, looked at the suit, shrugged and replaced it on the rack.

I was about to make a comment when I realised that it was beyond my budget anyway, so I just smiled back.

I stood there for a few moments, watching as the tall, elegant figure moved away and insinuated itself among the racks of clothes.

I was totally stunned. I mean... that figure!

I would give ten years of my life for a figure like that.

But... well, you know me... I'm not the envious type. No, really, I'm not! Well... all right then. But not envy. Honest-to-god jealousy! And, honestly, you would have felt the same.

I mean... you would not be-lieve it.

Every single item she picked up suited her to a T. She could have twisted an old rugger sock around her head and it would have looked exquisite.

Jet black hair. Dyed, of course. I'd have put money on it. Natural, she'd look twenty years older. Well... ten, anyway.

She picked up a chiffon scarf. Purple!

Not a colour I would have chosen but... well... She looked at it for a few moments then let it fall back onto the rack and picked up another in lime green, wrinkled her nose at it and walked on.

I was simply fascinated by the woman's taste and her... well... there's just no other word for it. Sheer elegance.

Eventually, though, I did manage to divert my attention, but there was nothing remotely suitable, especially on the clearance stand, so I picked up my bag and looked around for something else, and my eye fell on a smart trouser suit. I took it over to the mirror and held the jacket up in front of me.

It looked quite promising—until I spotted the two pale, chubby excuses for legs that hung below it.

The label in the jacket said size fourteen, short.

Wouldn't you just know it. The trousers would probably be right for length but there was no way my size sixteen bits were going to fit into it.

All right, eighteen, then... but small!

I was about to look for a larger size when I caught sight of the tall woman in the mirror.

To my amazement, she was busy concealing a variety of items about her person while the security camera was pointing the other way.

She looked up, caught my eye and actually winked at me, then she smoothed down her dress and turned to leave.

I was absolutely flabbergasted at what I had just seen so, of course, I followed her...

I watched her, cool as you like, speak to one of the assistants before leaving the shop and vanishing into the crowd outside.

I was wondering why the alarm hadn't sounded when a voice from behind nearly scared the life out of me. It was a security guard who was looking at me very strangely.

I felt as though I'd done something dreadful. I toyed with the idea of telling him what I'd just seen, but I really didn't want to get involved, so I said that I was just leaving.

I grabbed my bag from where I'd left it and headed for the exit.

Then, as I reached the door, the alarm went off and my way was blocked by the security guard and a short, blond woman.

As you can imagine, I was mortified. I hadn't done anything to set off the alarm, but protesting my innocence only made matters worse.

Well... long story short... the blond woman was the store manager.

She told me a customer had said that she saw me put something in my bag and suggested they keep an eye on me.

I tried to tell them what I'd seen but it was no use, and I really couldn't blame them. After all, a pretty face is far more readily believed than a homely one.

There I was, trying to pin the blame for my predicament on Miss Chelsea Two Thousand and... whatever. I mean... What would you have thought?

But I was not about to be called a thief if I could help it! I almost threw my bag onto the desk and told them to see for themselves.

I suppose I was expecting the manager to simply believe me and just hand it back, but she upended it over the desk and out fell my lipstick, compact, hairbrush, nail polish—and several large plastic buttons.

The security chap gathered them up and said, "Well, she was obviously a professional. They carry things for removing security tags. She must've dropped them into your bag to set the alarm off." Then he added, "You really shouldn't leave it lying around, madam…"

Well, really! Anyone would think it was my fault!

Of course, I accepted their apology. Rather graciously, I thought, under the circumstances.

So I decided to treat myself to the suit after all.

Credit where it's due, though, the staff bent over backwards to help me find just the right outfit.

I told them about the one that I'd almost lost to the other woman and, as I'd hoped, they found one in my size and they let me have it for an absolute song.

I've been simply dying to show it off to someone. I think I did awfully well. Don't you?

But, I must say that, if I *had* bet on that dyed hair, I would certainly have lost my money.

Silly me. Of course, it wasn't dyed. It was a wig. A very good one, though, I have to say…

And as for that watch…

Much too rich for my blood, of course, but

I... well... I *really* never expected to see it again.

Oh, no, Angela darling, please don't cry.

I really am so terribly sorry that Aiden recognised me when I arrived but, somehow, I don't think he'll be taking you to dinner tonight. ♦

The Hand of Glory

Amos Ketch chuckled as he opened the box.

Black and shriveled, the Hand of Glory lay as it had lain since his ancestor Jake Ketch was hanged for robbery three-hundred years ago.

Amos read the words again. The ink, black against age-brown vellum, had faded with the centuries. It described the pickling and baking of the hand of a recently hanged criminal, and the rendering down of fat from the corpse to make the black candle, clutched between its fingers.

Amos doubted that the grisly heirloom was genuine, let alone possessed of diabolical powers. He was only interested in its use.

"Recite these words while the candle burns," he read. "'Let all who sleep, sleep. Let all who are awake, be awake.' None within shall stir until the flame be extinguished."

Amos shuddered at the ancient words then chuckled again. Not that he actually believed, of course, but it *was* worth a try.

A glance at the clock told him it was well past midnight.

Mrs Kennedy, his landlady, was an unbelievably light sleeper and would awaken as soon as his foot touch the first stair. Even now, a year after the war, she was convinced that the enemy would invade and murder her in her bed.

Amos struck a match and applied it to the stump of black candle.

"Let all who sleep, sleep. Let all who are awake, be awake," he intoned, confident that nothing would happen, but fearful that something might.

Moments passed. He started up the stairs, then, hearing nothing from Mrs Kennedy, Amos knocked heavily on her door. Still nothing.

He turned the handle and looked in. The landlady lay motionless, her toothless mouth open, caught in mid-snore.

Amos panicked. Rushing back downstairs, he tried unsuccessfully to blow out the candle. The flame continued to flicker dimly. Nor did smothering it with a wet cloth have any effect. In desperation, Amos emptied the milk jug over the flame—which, obediently, went out.

Immediately, there was a sound from upstairs and Mrs Kennedy called down, "Is that you, Mr Ketch?"

He shoved the Hand into a drawer as there was a knock at the door.

"Sorry, Mrs Kennedy." he tried to look sheepish, "I'm sorry if I disturbed you. I've just upset the milk."

"Have you been upstairs? I woke up and my door was open."

"Me? No. Why would I? I fell asleep reading," Amos lied glibly.

"I couldn't have shut it properly, then. Must have been a draught."

Muttering to herself, Mrs Kennedy returned to her bed, leaving Amos already planning his next step.

He soon got over his qualms about using this evil device, and eagerly followed newspaper accounts of his robberies with great satisfaction, As village after village fell victim to his greed, he congratulated himself on the brilliance of his plan. In the city, the flickering candle might have caused suspicion, but not in remote country villages where electricity was virtually non-existant.

But, eventually, even Amos began to feel that it was time to retire and enjoy his ill-gotten gains. There was no pattern to the villages circled on his map. he had made sure of that. No sense telling the police where he was going to strike next. The Hand of Glory only affected those inside the house. It would never do to get nicked by police waiting outside.

He studied the map for several minutes then circled a small village about forty miles away.

"How very appropriate," he chuckled. "Moneywell!"

Amos parked his car in a copse on the hillside, he studied the village.

"Thirty-one houses and a pub," he thought, ignoring the church which stood in a field some distance away. "Be all right for a few quid."

As usual, the first few houses presented no problem. Amos made his entry, setting the Hand on a convenient table or ledge.

"Let all who sleep, sleep. Let all who are awake, be awake."

The incantation now warranted only lip service, and he no longer checked that the occupants were asleep. Nothing would disturb them.

Amos ignored jewellery and other valuables completely. They were traceable. Cash was not.

Stuffing his pockets with whatever cash he could lay his hands on, he extinguished the candle with milk from an eyedropper and left each house by the way he had entered.

At the seventh house, Amos completed his search only to find that the eyedropper was empty. He shrugged. There must be milk somewhere.

Placing the Hand on a small shelf, he tried the kitchen cupboard. Opening it required a fairly hefty tug and, as it swung back, there was a splash. The flame flickered, and a foul stench rose from the Hand.

Dismayed, Amos realised that he had knocked it into the bowl of a small shrine. As he watched by its own guttering light, the Hand dissolved completely leaving only the stump of black candle.

Amos had never considered the effect of Holy Water on the Hand and, too late, grabbed at the candle which promptly went out. Alone in the dark, and no longer protected by the Hand, Amos panicked.

Snatching up his loot, he stumbled across the room and out of the window. Missing his footing in the darkness, he landed spread-eagled on the soft earth beneath the window and staggered to his feet. Before he was able to regain his balance, handcuffs were snapped onto his wrists.

"Well. it 'ad to be a stranger. didn't it, Your Honour.'

The Constable's chest swelled as he faced the Magistrate.

"Stands to reason, don' it? The Verger wouldn't need no candle now, would 'e. I mean... not with 'im being blind an' all." ♦

Alarm

"So you think that I had something to do with Cartland's death, Inspector?"

Glyn Thompson turned away from the large aquarium that stood in the centre of his lounge. Tossing an empty fish-food packet into the waste paper basket, he faced his accuser.

"Proof?"

"Enough." The tall, plain-clothed man shrugged. "You don't mind if we have a look around do you, sir? I mean... I could wait here while my colleague goes for a search warrant..."

"Go right ahead, Inspector. I've nothing to hide."

"Then as you've no objection, sir, we'll start with the safe, shall we."

The tall man signaled to his burly companion.

Thompson spun the dials of his safe. As the door clicked open, strong hands grabbed him from behind, bundling him roughly into a chair. His arms were forced around behind the chair and tied together.

The 'inspector' laughed dryly.

"Don't feel too bad, Mr Thompson. Your partner fell for it, too. Oh, yes! He's dead. Well, I mean, he is... now. If you'd done the job properly, we wouldn't have tumbled your little game. Of course, we had to finish him off once he'd told us that you'd taken the ice."

"Ice?"

"Show him, Titch."

Thompson gasped for breath as a large, nicotine-stained hand came from behind, forcing his chin upwards, tilting the chair back until he was looking into Titch's snarling face.

"Yeah, ice... Sparklers... Diamonds. Call 'em what you like."

The words were accompanied by a blast of evil smelling breath.

"We know you've got 'em – or do you wanna end up like your mate?"

The back of the chair ground into Thompson's spine as the pressure increased. Then he was knocked to the ground and kicked in the ribs.

The tall man was asking if he'd had enough, then he was dragged across the room and hauled to his feet.

"Right! You want it the hard way..."

Thompson struggled to hold his breath as his head was thrust into the aquarium. His lungs felt painfully close to bursting when, without warning, he was bowled over as the aquarium crashed to the floor.

Gasping and retching, Thompson saw

uniformed men struggling with the thugs in a mess of water, gravel, and flopping fish.

A police sergeant untied his wrists and helped him to sit up.

"You all right, sir? Looks as though we were just in time."

There was a shout as Titch broke away from his captors and drew a gun. Backing away, he slipped on the mess from the aquarium and crashed against the door.

The gun went off catching the tall man in the chest. He fell, forgotten by his captors as they leapt to disarm Titch before he could recover.

Thompson looked round at the dying villain, only to find himself looking into the muzzle of a revolver. He threw himself aside as a second shot sounded.

The bullet missed Thompson and caught Titch in the temple.
The next shot grazed Thompson's cheek. Another lodged in his shoulder.

He saw the tall man slump lifelessly to the floor, then he, too, crumpled into an unconscious heap.

The air smelled of soap and ether. There was a dull ache in his shoulder and his mouth was dry.

A medley of half-memories ran through his

mind. His bungled attack on Cartland, whom he had left for dead; his partner's second, fatal ordeal at the hands of the two villains; the demise of the villains themselves; and, of course, the diamonds—invisible among the gravel at the bottom of the aquarium.

It was perfect. With the two thugs out of the way, there was nothing to connect him with Cartland's death. On the available evidence, the insurance company would undoubtedly pay up.

He opened his eyes.

"Good job you've got that alarm fitted to your safe, Mr Thompson."

A police constable was sitting by the bedside.

"It tipped us off that the safe was being done, so our patrol chaps piled in. But I'm afraid your partner, Mr Cartland, wasn't so lucky. Those two must have found out about the diamonds that your company was transporting, beaten him into opening the office safe and then finished him off. They must have stashed the loot, then gone on to your place to see what else they could find."

The tranquillising effects of recent anaesthetic helped Thompson to conceal his relief. Now, it was only a matter of sorting out the gems from the wreckage of the aquarium and the insurance would take care of the customer's loss.

Ignoring the doctor's advice, Thompson discharged himself from the hospital, took a taxi back to his house and let himself in.

"Oh, you all right, dear?" Mrs Fairfax, the 'daily', appeared from the kitchen, wiping her hands on her apron.

"Why don't you pop up to bed," she continued, eyeing the sling under his jacket. "I'll bring you up a nice cup of tea."

Thompson nodded. Can't do much while she's here, anyway. he thought, opening the lounge door. The room was a shambles of piled-up furniture and bare parquet.

"My son came in earlier and took the carpet to the cleaners," went on Mrs Fairfax. "But I'm afraid your aquarium was ruined. He cleared up the mess and dumped it in the canal..."

Thompson was stunned. There was nothing he could say or do without incriminating himself. Disconsolately, went up stairs and sat on the edge of his bed.

After a few minutes, he picked up the telephone, dialed a number and asked for the Claims Department.

Slowly, he replaced the receiver and buried his face in his hands and his shoulders shook with every sob.

"There we are, dear," Mrs Fairfax came in with a tray of tea and biscuits. "You'll feel better soon..."

"That thieving swindler, Cartland, hadn't paid the insurance premium," he blurted. "He must have kept the money himself... I'm ruined. Those diamonds were worth over three million quid!"

Mrs Fairfax was flabbergasted.

"Oh! The villain!" she said. "However could he do such a dreadful thing to a nice gentleman like you?" ♦

<u>Almost with Love</u>

"But what else can I think?"

Mrs Kaplan dabbed away the hot emotion that stung her eyes.

"It was a photoh of Adolf Hitler. And, when he touched it, it was almost... almost with love."

Mrs Baines looked up from the pencil that she had rotated constantly between her fingers as she listened to the old lady's story.

"I can imagine how upsetting it must have been – particularly since you and Mr Waldenbrook have been so close. I'm sure there's a perfectly innocent explanation."

"Oh, but he must never find out. I couldn't bear him to think that I had been spying on him. I've been so very happy here, but I'm sure you understand why I have to leave. I'll remain in my room until I can make other arrangements."

The Warden dropped the pencil onto the desk and stood up.

"We'll all miss you a great deal. I do hope you'll reconsider."

Mrs Kaplan tucked her lace hanky into the sleeve of her cardigan.

"Perhaps if you would tell the other residents that I'm a little tired."

Mrs Baines made the announcement at

lunch. A slight chill. It was accepted. She was heading back along the hall towards her office when the tyres of Mr Waldenbrook's chair squeaked on the lino behind her.

"A moment please, Mrs Baines."

She turned, to be fixed with a friendly but piercing gaze over rimless half-lenses.

"Forgive me..." His voice dropped almost to a whisper as the chair rolled to a stop beside her.

"A chill? Maybe. But not of the body." He tapped his chest. "Of the heart, perhaps."

Mrs Baines rummaged for the right words.

The old man raised a hand.

"No. I understand. A pale fiction. A white lie. But perhaps a few words in your office."

The old man turned his chair towards the window and looked across the lawn to where the path sloped gently down towards the rocky cove.

"I was leaving my room this morning when Mrs Kaplan left your office." He paused. "I have never known her to use the back staircase before and, since she would have had to pass only me to reach the main staircase, I have concluded that I have unwittingly had a part to play in the development of this sudden chill..."

Mrs Baines flushed.

"Some bad news regarding a very dear

friend, Mr Waldenbrook," Another... what had he called it? A pale fiction. "She wants to be on her own for a while."

"Twelve years I have known Rebecca Kaplan. Of respect, there have been many things that we have never discussed—many questions that have remained unasked. But secrets? No." He placed both hands on the arms of the wheelchair. "In this, I cannot climb the stairs to ask what is wrong, but I am sure that you already have that knowledge."

There was no room to manoeuvre around the implied question. The grey eyes studied her closely.

"I'm sorry, Mr Waldenbrook. If Mrs Kaplan wishes to stay in her room there is little that we can do."

The old man's pale cheeks reddened, and moisture shone in the corners of his eyes. Despite his broad shoulders, he suddenly looked small and frail.

"Thank you," he said, simply.

He swung the chair expertly around and was gone.

Mrs Baines was preparing afternoon tea when there was an insistent hammering on the back door.

"Come quick, missus." A young boy in bathing trunks stood gasping on the step.

"There's a man fallen in the sea."

Just round a bend in the path, Mr Waldenbrook's wheelchair was wedged precariously above water that swelled and gurgled over the rocks below. On the beach at the foot of the path, a small group gathered around the unconscious forms of Mr Waldenbrook and a tall youth. Both were fully clothed, and the youth was bleeding from a darkening graze over his right eye.

"What happened?"

The boy pointed up at the wheelchair.

"He fell out. I couldn't do nothing, so I run for help."

The wail of an approaching siren claimed Mrs Baines' attention, bringing with it a flood of relief.

"He could have been killed... Did you see that cut?... Ought to get a medal, pulling the old man out like that."

The air was filled with animated opinions as the unconscious men were swathed in red blankets and carried up to the waiting ambulance.

The residents were understandably concerned about the incident and continually asked whether there was any news from the hospital. Mrs Kaplan, now apparently recovered from her feigned indisposition, sat apart from the others and did not join in the general speculation.

At last, Mrs Baines called for their attention. Mr Waldenbrook, she assured them, was none the worse for his adventure and was sleeping peacefully.

"The young man…" She struggled to make herself heard above the excited chatter. "The young man has undergone an operation but he's going to be all right. We have a lot to thank him for. But for his brave and unselfish act, Mr Waldenbrook would almost certainly have died."

Heads nodded appreciatively.

"Mr Waldenbrook will be back tomorrow."

In the privacy of the Warden's office, Mrs Kaplan readily agreed to resume her normal relationship with Mr Waldenbrook on his return.

"I hadn't realised how very much I must have hurt him. From my room, I can see most of the way down the path to the beach. I saw him steer his chair towards the edge." Tears traced the lines of age down the old lady's cheeks. "When it stopped at the edge, he lifted himself with both hands and threw himself over."

Mrs Baines tried to comfort her.

"I'm sure it was just an unfortunate accident, nothing more. He simply lost control and was thrown out.”

Excited faces filled every window as an ambulance arrived the following afternoon. Mr Waldenbrook, was carefully transferred to his chair. Waving away further assistance, he thanked the ambulance crew and rolled his chair up the entrance ramp towards his room.

By tea-time, Fairlands was once more filled with whispered speculation and an expectant silence fell as tyres squeaked in the hall and Mr Waldenbrook glided to his usual place. He peered over his spectacles at the expectant faces.

“Good afternoon,” he said quietly, raising his hands in mock horror at the deluge of questions that resulted.

“An unfortunate accident. And thank you, yes, I am very glad to be back.” He coated a triangle of buttered bread with a delicate layer of strawberry jam. The matter was closed.

Later that afternoon, Mrs Baines was carefully stacking the dishwasher when the front door-bell rang.

“Good evening.” An elderly man raised his battered trilby. “I believe there’s a Mr... Waldenbrook, is it?... staying here? I’ve just come from the hospital.”

The man took out a photograph and

pressed in into her hands. The picture was of a young man in conversation with Adolf Hitler at an official gathering.

"That is him, isn't it?"

Mrs Baines held the door open.

"I think you'd better come in."

In the lounge, Mr Waldenbrook barely glanced at the picture.

"I thought I recognised you at the hospital," the man said. "The name clinched it. Even though you've anglicised it. Pieter Waldenbroek. Berlin. My first big assignment as a cub reporter."

Mrs Kaplan put her hands to her face, stifling a gasp.

"Please!" Mr Waldenbrook touched her arm gently and glided from the room.

He returned carrying on his lap a polished wooden box. From under the box, he produced a larger copy of the same photograph, which he handed to Mrs Kaplan.

"I was aware that someone was watching. I would have explained, but you had retired to your room. I could not ask anyone else to explain for me. I wanted to think, so I went down the path where we have talked so often. Then the accident happened, and it is no longer a private matter."

He pointed to the image of a young man, almost obscured behind the image of Hitler.

"This is the only picture that I have of my brother, Franz. Yesterday was the sixtieth anniversary of his death in 1945. Now, if you will excuse me..."

He placed the box on the table and left the room.

"They fought in the Resistance. He almost died in the explosion that killed his brother. He has been in that wheelchair ever since."

The reporter opened the box and took out a large gold medal bearing the Olympic symbol and read the inscription aloud.

"'Pieter Waldenbroek. 1000 metres Freestyle. Berlin, 1936'. He was just fourteen."

There were gasps of amazement as he held up the medal for them to see.

"Oh, but you can't..." Mrs Baines began. "He wouldn't want..."

The reporter smiled.

"No, of course not. As a young boy, it took tremendous courage to fight in the Resistance. Yesterday he showed that he still has that courage, and, thanks to that wheelchair, he still has powerful shoulders. I came here today to thank the man who saved my grandson from drowning." ◆

Train of Thought

I was far too preoccupied with my own discomfort to cast more than a passing glance at the woman who had taken the far end seat opposite. It had been some years since I had given serious thought to the opposite sex. To me, fast approaching retirement, youngsters nowadays were like beings from another age. There was no romance any more. Sex, yes. It was all around. The world was full of allusion to it...

Suddenly realising that my train of thought had taken an unusual turn, I looked around the carriage. The large man beside me shifted his position, allowing me to arrange myself more comfortably. As I did so, the train jolted and drew away from the dimly-lighted platform outside.

The woman opposite stood up to remove her overcoat and place it on the rack above her head. From my seated position, her mature form was silhouetted momentarily against the light from the corridor. Her white blouse tightened as she reached up, accentuating the shape of her breasts, suggesting a firmness unusual in a woman of her advancing years.

I turned my head casually away towards the window, hoping that my inexplicable interest had not been apparent to my fellow passengers.

A light drizzle began to speckle the glass. Soon, tiny silver rivulets began to form, and I watched them move slowly towards the back of the pane, swept by the slipstream.

Anticipation of the long journey ahead and fatigue from an even longer day's exertions started to take their toll and I drifted into sleep.

Some time later, the rhythm of the wheels was interrupted as the train passed at speed over a number of points in quick succession, rocking me into wakefulness.

Unaware of the train having stopped at any stations, I was surprised to see that the woman and I were now alone in the compartment. Her eyes were firmly fixed on something just along the corridor, as though totally unaware of my existence. I found myself once again studying her.

In profile, her face was strong, yet with a softness that I had not noticed before. It seemed for a moment as though I detected a hint of loneliness in her pensive expression. Her shoulders rose slightly as she took a deep, silent breath and let it out slowly as though to acknowledge the accuracy of my speculation. A mild embarrassment that suddenly rose in me subsided at the realisation that she could not possibly have known of my fleeting thought. I turned my eyes towards the dark world outside.

Minutes passed. My earlier tiredness had now become reverie and my attention was once again drawn back to the woman, whose reflection stood out starkly against the night that lay beyond the window.

Since there were only the two of us in the compartment, it was not unnatural that, eventually, her head turned slowly in my direction.

Intrigued by the effect that her presence was having on me. I let my eyelids droop as though from fatigue and began to study her reflection from beneath them.

A sudden jolt as the train clattered across more points made me open my eyes and the woman's reflection leapt into sharp focus.

Instinctively, I looked in her direction. In the glare of the flickering light, moisture sparkled at the corners of her eyes and, for a moment, it seemed that we were bonded by a pang of loneliness. She smiled gently as though she understood then turned to look along the corridor again.

The pain of that moment remained with me and I wondered if she had somehow felt it too. I ached to make conversation but the innate shyness that protected me from embarrassing encounters also prevented me, despite considerable success in business, from forming personal attachments.

But somewhere deep inside, I knew that this was my one chance, and that Fate had brought together two lonely souls.

No word had passed between us but I knew that I could love this woman.

For several minutes, my pulse raced as I struggled to overcome my reticence. Then, almost composed, I was about to speak when the loudspeaker crackled a warning that we were approaching the last station and that we should be sure to take our belongings with us. The message seemed to shatter the promising illusion that I had allowed myself.

The woman stood and reached up for her coat. I, too, stood and took down my briefcase. As the train drew into the station, its slow swaying caused our hands to touch.

In that moment, my illusion became reality. I was stunned by the closeness of her. I wanted to cry out, to tell her of my feelings, but the words would not come. I stood unable to move as she stepped into the corridor and left the train.

A few moments later, as she passed the window of the carriage where I was still standing, she looked up at me.

She smiled, a sincere smile that touched me unimaginably deeply, and I saw her lips form a single whispered phrase. "Thank you."

Suddenly, my hesitation had vanished. I smiled back, picked up my belongings and followed her out onto the platform. ◆

The Visitors

Trask and Hempel took five. It had been a long trek up the mountain from the tracking station.

Trask, tall with an air of authority, sat on a large boulder and looked back down the way they had come. Six hours, he thought, and still nothing.

His companion, Hempel, a thick-set man with a permanent hang-dog expression, started to take off his rucksack. He stopped, poised with his arms half out of the straps. His nostrils quivered and twitched like a hungry fox sampling the scent of its forthcoming kill.

"Hey, boss," he grunted, with all the panache of a punch-drunk pug. "Thought you said there weren't no-one up here. Sure ain't no animal doin' that cookin'."

Trask sniffed. There was a faint but appetising aroma drifting down the mountain on the light breeze.

Suddenly, dust spurted from the track in front of his feet and the sharp crack of the rifle shot ricocheted around the hills.

Before they had a chance to move, a spindly, bewhiskered figure emerged from the underbrush some fifty yards further up the track. The ancient rifle slung across his shoulders looked harmless enough. Certainly, the shot had not originated from there.

The man spat.

"Howdy," he drawled. "Kind'a strayed a mite for city folks, ain't yer?"

Trask stood up. A second shot splintered the rock behind him. The hidden gunman could just as easily pick both of them off.

"That's my boy. We ain't used to strangers here'bouts." The hillbilly spat again. "An' we don't cotton to folks what sneaks up on a body."

"We were not sneaking up," protested Trask. "We're looking for a... an aircraft... that came down near here last night. We work at the radar station across the valley."

The hillbilly grinned, broken yellow teeth showing dully through his bushy whiskers.

"It's okay, Zeke. They speaks too ed'cated to be McWhirters."

Trask was thankful that Hempel rarely spoke.

A muscular giant of a man with a baby face appeared from the scrub.

"Aw! Shucks, paw," he pleaded, "Cain't I jest wing 'em a mite? If'n we let 'em go, they sure as hell gonna tell them McWhirters where we's at."

His pa frowned.

"Where's your manners, boy? That there ain't no way to treat our dinner guests..."

Trask would have declined the invitation,

but for the ancient rifle that now pointed straight at him in a manner somewhat less than casual. He'd heard rumours about some of these hill folk and their strange diet. He swallowed his revulsion. The smell was far more appetising than he would have expected.

"We'd be glad to dine with you, Mr... er...?"

"Jed Clay. Ah 'pologises for my boy. He's jest bin a mite suspicious of ever'one since his maw died. We got a custom hereabouts that it don't do to trust no one till he's joined you in a dish of possum belly and hominy grits." The rifle moved ominously despite the smile. "And we don't want to break no tradition now..."

By the time the group reached the ramshackle dwelling, any reservations were finally dispelled by hunger. They ate in silence.

The meal over, Hempel leaned across to Trask.

"What about the ship?" He rasped in a stage whisper.

Jed Clay's shaggy left eyebrow went up.

"Ship?"

Trask made haste to correct Hempel's slip.

"Er... the... er... plane..." he said calmly. "The one I mentioned. We sometimes call them 'ships'."

Anyway, if he did try to explain about the spaceship, they wouldn't understand. And, as for visitors from another world...

"Dangbust it! That must be the hunk of metal that come down in back of the big rock. Can't say as I'm surprised it come down. Ain't never seen no airyplane without wings afore." Zeke was obviously not as dumb as he looked. "I seen it this morning, paw. All big and shiny and..."

"Can you take us there?" Trask hoped that Zeke had been too scared to go near the thing.

The ambassadors from Antares had chosen to land in this unpopulated area and expected only Trask and his companion to greet them. What if they mistook Zeke for their welcoming committee. There was no telling how they might react if suddenly faced by his rifle.

Jed belched loudly. "Sure he can. T'aint but a step away."

Just over the brow of the hill, the spaceship glinted in the sun. It had landed so softly that the ground beneath it was hardly indented, despite its great weight. The smooth sphere was devoid of any markings or openings.

From his many communications with the Antareans over the past months, Trask knew that this was a technology thousands of years ahead of anything on Earth.

While Hempel set up the automatic translator on its tripod, Trask went into the clearing to examine the craft. It seemed to be alive with power, as though ready for instant departure should there be any sign of trouble. The whole globe was humming softly. Trask went back to the others and switched on the translator. It crackled for a moment, then fell silent.

Trask spoke briefly into the microphone.

No reply. He tried again. Still nothing.

After a few more fruitless attempts. He crossed the clearing again and walked around the base of the great craft.

He was about to make his way back to try the translator again when he spotted a small dark patch on the ground a short distance away.

He touched it.

It was blood—and fairly fresh at that.

A trail of spots led back around the ship into the shadow of the big rock that towered above. There were some smears on the shining metal, indicating that there must be an entrance at this point, low down near the ground. He almost ran back to the others.

"Zeke," he rapped, "did you loose off a shot at anyone up here like you did as we came up the trail?"

The big man glanced sheepishly at his pa for guidance.

Jed looked angry.

"Dang bust it, Zeke, if you done shoot someone and hid it from your paw, you's in a heap o' trouble, boy..."

"Aw, shucks, paw," Zeke protested. "You knows I ain't never shot at no one 'ceptin' to scare em a mite—less'n they was McWhirters..."

He brightened.

"Guess that must have been the possum ah winged this morning. Ah got one fair and square, but the other skedaddled round in back o' that their machine afore I could get it again. That was just before afore that hummin' started. Darndest thing I ever seen."

Trask went hot, then cold. "What did it look like?"

Zeke shrug his massive shoulders.

"Same as always, I guess," he said. "'Ceptin' for the green fur. But I sure as hell got the other one," he added proudly.

Dejectedly, Trask helped Hempel pack the translator away. He wondered if the wounded ambassador had been able to send a warning message back to Antares before he died.

In gloomy silence, they started back down the hill.

Behind them, the voice of Zeke could be heard pleading with his pa.

"Shucks, paw. What'd I do wrong? A body's gotta eat, don't he?" ♦

No Tears for Tomorrow

That old gate still needs mending. Well, there never seemed to be much point in putting it right. Molly always laughed when I promised to mend it one day when there was nothing more important to think about. Anyway, the kids'd only have had it off his hinges again with their swinging on it.

I don't suppose that's changed much, anyway. The times I had to chase them off over the years you wouldn't believe. Off up the lane they'd go back to the estate. Sometimes they'd blow raspberries and thumb their noses at me, and off they'd run laughing at how clever and grown-up they thought they were being.

Grown-up? Of course, most of them are now. Kids of their own, I shouldn't wonder. Probably out there now swinging on someone else's gate. Best let it sit there, locked in by that strip of grass sticking out from underneath. Devil of a job to keep that trimmed. Molly used to keep on at me till I took the shears to it. She was happy then.

Still, I suppose I wasn't so much different from those kids in my younger days. Mind you, we had a different set of standards – respect for our elders, for a start – but we liked a bit of fun just the same. It was always quiet in the village. The highlight of the year was the church's Social on the Saturday after the Harvest Festival.

That's where I met my Molly for the first time. I knew who she was, of course. After all, we'd both been brought up in a small community. But I'd never actually met her to speak to, like. It didn't do to take too much interest in the farmer's daughter when your dad was only his stockman. Not until you were properly introduced, and I couldn't see that ever happening.

So there we were at this Social sitting on opposite sides of the room from each other. Suddenly she looks across at me and smiles.

Well, I thought my heart was never going to stop thumping. I got so wound up, I was across that floor asking her to dance afore I had time to think about it. I took her by the hand and we were out there on the dance floor before you could say 'knife'. Just then the record came to an end and the vicar's wife said it was time for refreshments.

That was lucky, that was. I bought two cups of tea and we shared a plate of old Mrs Wymark's home-made biscuits until the music started again. We didn't say much during the break. At least, I don't think so. But I mind the way Molly looked up at me when I bowed stiffly and asked if she'd care to dance.

"Thank you," she said, "but I don't

quickstep. I hope you don't mind. Perhaps we could try the next waltz." Then she added, "if that's all right with you, Daniel."

My young heart was still thumping. "That will be just fine."

Then I realised what she'd said. She called me 'Daniel'. I reckon that's the sweetest thing that ever happened to me.

Of course, it was all right about the quickstep. I didn't quickstep either. And I didn't waltz or foxtrot for that matter. In my eagerness to make a good impression, it slipped my mind that I didn't actually know how to dance. My cheeks started to feel warm.

"I... er... I'll just take the cups back," I blurted. It was just the excuse I needed to give me time to think.

I'd almost made it to the paper doily-covered trestle table when someone bumped against me and the cups shot out of my hand.

Apologising profusely to Mrs Wymark, I scrambled around picking up the pieces of broken china, and limped back to where Molly was waiting.

"Oh dear! Are you all right, Daniel?" Her soft brown eyes were wide like a six-week-old calf's. I wanted to tell her, but the limp needed a lot of concentration.

"I must've tripped," I said, wondering who I had to thank for giving me the excuse I needed. "I'm afraid I don't think I'll be able to have that waltz with you now though, Miss Molly."

"No matter," she said. Then, leaning close enough for me to smell the freshness of her long brown hair, she whispered, "I don't really waltz, either."

We both laughed quietly, and the sound passed between us like an unspoken betrothal. The limp quickly became a new spring in my step as I followed her back to her seat, and I knew that there could never be anyone else.

We used to do our courting by the stream at the bottom of the Long Meadow. Of course, that's been gone these twenty years now, ever since they started building the estate. The stream goes down through a pipe and comes out on the other side of the road nowadays. I remember how upset we were when the bulldozers moved in.

Up till then, of course, we still had our picnics and Sunday outings down there. We'd sit there on the grass not saying a lot but just being together – or watching the kingfisher catching his family's supper. He'd perch on a branch where the sunlight coming down through the trees dappled the water as it ran between the rocks. Suddenly, there'd be a flurry of silver and blue and he'd be off and away upstream to his nest with a tasty big fish in his beak.

One day, about a year after the wedding it'd be, we were down there watching him when Molly suddenly looked at me kind of strange.

I could see she was near bursting to tell me something.

"D'you suppose he's got many young mouths to feed, Daniel?"

I laughed. "Quite a few I expect," I said, wondering what she was leading up to. Then it clicked, and my heart started pounding.

"When? When's it to be?" And before I had a chance to ask whether she thought it would be a boy or a girl, she put her fingers up to my lips to silence my excited, stupid questions.

"It's not certain yet," she said softly, stroking the side of my face with one finger. "But, as near as I can make out, sometime in February, I reckon."

I felt as though I'd just set one foot in Heaven. There was nothing could have made us happier. We made such plans, you wouldn't believe it. Choosing names and such. But it wasn't to be.

I was working in the forge one day when a young lad came in with a message to get home right away. By the time I got there, Molly had lost the baby. Slipped over in the snow the doctor said. Just outside by the front door. She must've been lying there quite a time before

Mrs Newsome, the postmistress, came by to deliver a letter and found her. The doctor took me aside and said there was a chance that Molly wouldn't be able to have any more children. Truth to tell, I was so thankful that Molly was all right that—well, it was disappointing but there it was. Still, as it happened we didn't have much time to brood over it even if we'd wanted to.

About a week later, Constable Parkin, the bobby from the next village, came by on his bike to tell everyone that Poland had been invaded and we were at war. We'd heard talk in the village that some pretty unpleasant things were happening in the world outside but, of course, we never thought that we'd be personally involved. Then I remembered about the letter I'd stuck behind the clock when we'd had to have the doctor for Molly. It was from the War Office.

They were long years from then on. We wrote as often as we could, and it did my heart good to know that Molly was waiting for me back home. I met quite a few chaps who weren't that lucky, so I counted my blessings and looked forward to it all being over. I'd never spent Christmas away from home before and six of them passed in lonely succession before it ended. In fact, it was about a week before the seventh Christmas that my train finally pulled in to the station. I should have written to let Molly know when I'd be home but I hadn't known myself until thirty-six hours before, and I'd been travelling since then.

The platform was empty except for a porter and an American airman who almost missed the train.

He ran past, loaded with luggage, almost bowling me over as I trudged up the steps of the bridge.

"Gee! Sorry, Mac…" He shouted back at me over his shoulder, and we both laughed when he nearly fell over his case.

Reaching the platform, he ran alongside the slowly moving train, wrenched open a door, threw his luggage inside and scrambled in after it. Leaning out to grab window strap he slammed the door shut and, caught sight of me following his progress from the iron overbridge. He gave me a cheery wave. I waved back and grinned, then the engine passed under the bridge, enveloping me in a cloud of steam.

It was good to be back in familiar surroundings. The country lanes hadn't changed at all except for the season. Although I wanted to get back to the cottage and see my Molly again, I found the walk exhilarating. I could pick up the rest of my luggage from the station tomorrow, but I'd remembered to put

Molly's present in my case and I couldn't wait to see the look on her face when she saw it.

I stood outside for a couple minutes before going in. There was a thin plume of smoke rising from the chimney and the air was filled with the smell of cooking, I left my case where it was and went in.

The door was slightly ajar, and I could see Molly with her back to me, tending to the meal she was cooking on the range. I was so happy to be home, I felt fit to burst.

"Hello, Molly, darling" I said, pushing the door wide and letting the light pour in from the weak winter sun.

For a moment, she stood without moving, as though the sound of my voice had turned her to stone. Then, slowly, she put down the spoon she was using and, lifting her apron, she wiped her hands as she turned around.

"Oh, Molly!"

The words spilled out, drawn by the pain of disbelief and the confirming tears that were tracing their way down her cheeks.

Dropping the apron that did nothing to hide her advanced pregnancy, Molly put her hands up to her face and turned away.

I was numb. The room seemed suddenly too small. I had to get away, to find space. To think.

I wanted to hide from this reality—to escape

into the excited anticipation just a moment gone. My thoughts raced, tripping over each other in their desperation to make sense.

By the time I'd gathered them into a reasonable bundle, I was sitting by the stream in Parson's Field. It wasn't the same as the days we'd spent all those years ago courting in the Long Meadow, but I sat there just watching a sandpiper stepping and probing between the icy rocks.

It reminded me of the kingfisher in Long Meadow a lifetime ago. But how carefree and uncomplicated the sandpiper's life must be, I thought. Wintering here and then flying back to breed in the cooler northern countries when spring comes. No ties. No lasting relationships. But wasn't that what had always set us apart from the animals. The gift of caring. Of loving and being loved. I'd seen men die because that gift had been taken from them.

There was a chap in my squad, same age as me. Jack Ruskin, his name was. Been made up to corporal the day before. When his letter arrived, he couldn't wait to read it. Then I saw his expression change and he just sat there, staring out across the desert. After a while he screwed the letter into a ball dropped it. He watched it roll away and started muttering something to himself over and over. Suddenly, he stood up, clenching his fists. He took in a deep breath and shouted, "Bloody Yanks" at the top of his voice. Then he turned and disappeared over the top of the sand dune, straight into a minefield.

I thought of the American airman at the station. He'd seemed friendly enough. Left in a strange country while all the local men were away fighting a war. Perhaps too friendly.

So much had happened in the past few years to change the world. People too. It was difficult to imagine how the people we left behind must've felt. But even on a battlefield—especially on the battlefield—the need to be needed is strong. Out there, surrounded by the noise and the blood and the smell of fear, where the living and the dead are separated by instant oblivion or an eternity of pain, it provided the will to go on.

That need had brought me home. But, here in the quiet solitude of the valley, might not Molly's need have been just as great. There had been little enough time to think about much more than surviving out there. How would I have fared if I'd been the one left behind and with so much time to think?

Once the initial shock had passed, I became conscious of the growing dusk and a biting wind that stung my face with flecks of snow. The sandpiper had long since returned to its nest and so, I realised in a manner of speaking, must I.

There was nothing that I could say or do that was going to alter what had happened. Any pedestal can fall with time, and perhaps I'd built Molly's a bit too high. It had happened to so many others but, deep down inside, I'd always thought that my Molly was different. So few years had passed since we first met at that social. And so many of those years I'd been away. I was sure that my feelings hadn't been wrong then, and I couldn't believe that Molly's had been, either. Now it was up to us both to see if we couldn't put things right.

My case had gone from where I'd left it by the time I reach the cottage.

The moon was high in a clear, starry sky and the night was bitter cold. The surface of the lane sparkled with a new frost forming on the old. It crunched under my feet as I turned onto the garden path.

I lifted the latch and opened the door slowly. It creaked slightly as it had always done. The smell of cooking was now almost gone, replaced by the cosy smell from the brass oil lamp that shed its yellow light across Molly's hair and arms.

She sat at the far end of the whitewood table, her head cradled in her arms. A handkerchief, screwed up in one fist, told me she'd been crying before she fell asleep. I could hear her soft breathing as I gently closed the door. Better like this, I thought. We'd both feel better after a good night's sleep. I pulled a wheel-back chair away from the table and sat down. Just then the clock on the mantelpiece struck six and Molly stirred.

She started slightly when she saw me sitting there. Her eyes met mine for a moment before she hastily lowered them. This close to the lamp, I'd have to be blind not to have noticed how swollen they were. Slowly, she raised them again and looked into mine.

"I didn't know how to tell you," she said eventually, her voice trembling and broken. "Oh, Daniel, whatever must you be thinking."

She gave way to a shuddering sigh, burying her face in her hands while her shoulders shook silently. I just sat, clouded with tears and unable to speak, just hurting at seeing her so unhappy.

Unable to bear it any longer, I stood up and pulled her to me. It was so good to hold her again that nothing else seemed to matter. Her gentle sobbing gradually eased, and she wiped her eyes and looked up at me.

"He was lonely and so far from home," she said. "I didn't love him. I couldn't love anyone else. Only you. You must believe that."

Somehow, despite everything, I'd never

doubted that. Not even for a moment.

"Then why, Molly?"

"Perhaps because I understood his loneliness. We needed each other and there was nothing wrong in needing someone. There was only friendship, nothing more. I know I should have told you. I tried. But it's not the same in a letter. The words don't mean the same no matter how hard you try. And I did try, so many times…" She paused, still breathing heavily.

I knew she was right.

What could she have told me in a letter that might not be misunderstood? How many others have misunderstood? Had Jack Ruskin died because of a simple misunderstanding?

"He was a perfect gentleman," Molly went on. "We had a deep respect for each other. He wrote to his wife and children in Poland every week, never even knowing whether his letters ever reached them. But always, he believed that they were still alive and thinking of him. He just wanted the war to end so that he could go back and find them. Then it did end, and we went into town for a drink to celebrate VE Day. That's when it happened. On the way home…" Her words failed, and she began to sob again.

I knew that I should be insane with rage or jealousy or something. But I was only conscious of the reassuring feel of Molly's hair.

It was soft to my touch, just the way it had been in the Long Meadow. The way I'd remembered it on cold nights in North Africa, in a rain-filled foxhole in Sicily, and all the way back across Europe.

Perhaps, I thought, it had been better to find out this way.

But what if the doctor had been right?

No. I knew that Molly would still have been honest with me. Someday—much later perhaps and in her own way—but she'd have told me the truth. Her pregnancy had only accelerated matters. But it also proved that the doctor had been wrong and, instead of feeling angry, I found myself thanking God for that. What was done was done and it would end, right here and now. If we were to have a future together, there must be no tears for tomorrow.

And, tomorrow, I had a gate to mend. ♦

The Passing Of Mr Feeney

I left the station just as the church clock struck eight, paused for a moment to check my watch, then crossed the road to Mr Feeney's shop on the corner opposite. I was alone in the street save for my own reflection in the large plate-glass window of the shop. The street was unusually devoid of traffic.

Upon entering, several seconds passed before my eyes adjusted to the gloom of the interior.

The light, which should have streamed in from the setting sun, was dimmed by mullioned windows. The familiar modern decor was gone, replaced by the brown-painted dinginess of age.

Closing the door, I looked out at the street. Through the small panes of poor-quality glass, was the bustle of a busy thoroughfare. The church clock showed four o'clock, and the fashions, even the buses and cars, were all out of date. It was a strange world to which I did not belong.

Sensing a movement behind me, I turned as a young man stepped forward to serve me. There was a certain familiarity about him; a close resemblance to the balding, arthritic little man who usually served here.

I moved towards him, about to enquire after

Mr Feeney. His knuckles whitened as he gripped the counter and regarded me with terror. Stepping back, he crossed himself

He tried to speak, threw out his hands as though to keep me away, then backed through a curtained doorway into the room beyond.

Mystified, I followed, intruding upon the privacy of a young woman who lay in childbirth on a bed in the corner. The young man knelt beside her. He clasped her hand to his cheek and prayed.

In the pale, flickering light of a single gas mantle, the girl was white, her dark hair mingling with the sweat that glistened on her face.

With each deep breath, her whole being shuddered with the effort to give birth to a reluctant child. Her eyes opened for a moment and met mine as I stood framed in the doorway.

She smiled faintly, as though in welcome, and sighed. Her eyes closed once more, her struggles grew weaker, then she lay still.

The young man's shoulders shook as the emotion poured from him and he turned unseeing eyes in my direction. Unable to console him in his grief, I went back into the shop.

I tossed a coin onto the counter and picked up my usual newspaper. The date leapt out at me and headlines screamed of happenings fifty years ago. The room spun, and blackness engulfed me.

Someone was shaking me by the arm.

"You all right, mate?"

A heavy, bull-necked man was leaning over me.

"Why... what...?"

All around was the clatter of the train.

"Gawd! You didn't half go a funny colour there for a minute, mate," the big man smiled ruggedly. "I thought you was gonna snuff it.'

He looked concerned.

"Sure you're all right now? Gawd, that must have been *some* dream you was 'aving."

If he had only known. I thought.

Pulling myself up from a slumped position. I straightened my jacket.

"Thank you. Yes. I'm fine now."

I felt the colour returning to my cheeks. Having no idea of the time, I glanced at my watch. It had stopped at four o'clock.

"Have we passed Richfield yet?"

"No, not yet, mate About another twenty minutes."

The big man pulled out a large hunter and flicked open the cover.

"We're running a bit late, as it goes. There y'are, mate! Spot-on with Big Ben, that is."

He held in out for me to set mine by.

I thanked him and settled back to watch the countryside speeding past, the train swaying gently in time with the rhythm of the wheels.

My watch had stopped at four o'clock.

I remembered my dream.

Leaving the station as the clock struck eight, I checked my watch. It was right. We must have caught up those lost minutes. Crossing the road to Mr Feeney's shop, I tried to shrug off a sense of foreboding. Could it be possible, at twenty-five, to experience a fifty-year-old dream?

It was reassuring to see the street reflected in the window. I reached the shop door convinced that it had indeed been a bad dream.

To my relief the setting sun bathed the whole interior with light, causing the modern decor to blaze with orange and crimson. *This* was the shop I knew. Through the door's single pane, the street looked just as it always did. The sense of relief was overwhelming.

"So you've come at last?"

The voice of Mr Feeney caused me to turn. He stood in his usual place behind the neatly arranged counter.

"Late?" I joked. "The last visitor of the day, perhaps, but never late."

"Last time, you came too soon, and you are rarely late. But, late or early, you must *always* be the last visitor."

I wondered what he meant by that.

As I stepped forward, Mr Feeney swayed slightly, and his gnarled hands gripped the counter. Then, just as the young man had done in my dream, he crossed himself and smiled weakly, his voice trembling.

"I've waited such a long time for you come again."

I followed as he hobbled painfully into the back room.

Taking down a photograph from the mantelpiece, he sat wheezily in an armchair. He turned the picture over and handed me a folded envelope that was taped to the back of the oval frame.

"I knew you would be here soon. I've been ready these fifty years."

The tenderness in his eyes moved me almost to tears as he caressed the picture gently. It was of the girl whom I had seen die in this very room.

"In all that time, she has never left my thoughts. Now, at last, we'll be together again."

He took a deep breath, clutched his chest, and slumped into my arms.

"'Ere you are, mate. Richfield." The big man's hand was on my shoulder.

Thanking him hastily, I grabbed my briefcase and umbrella and left the train.

Reaching for my season ticket as I hurried along the platform, my delving hand closed over a folded envelope in my pocket. I opened it to find the coin that I had tossed onto the counter. As soon as I saw the date on it, I knew how Mr Feeney had known that I would soon be back.

Even as I felt an overwhelming compassion for the little old man, I realised the terrible truth. Mr Feeney had been waiting for Death and, with my mind desperately refusing to accept that this was not a dream, I knew he had been waiting for me.

Showing my ticket to the man at the gate. I left the station and looked up at the church clock. It was a quarter past eight.

Across the street, the window offered no reflection of me. The great frame was empty, save for the clear reflection of a young couple with a newborn baby, alone in the street. I watched them greet each other.

I hesitated at the door of the shop. With the passing of Mr Feeney, there seemed little point in my going in and, in that moment, I knew that I would never—could never—enter the shop again.

As I turned to leave, I glimpsed a movement in the doorway and saw a tall figure, hooded and cowled, reflected in the glass.

I shuddered and averted my eyes. Unwilling to look again, I crossed myself and walked hurriedly away down the empty street. ♦

The Hand of Friendship

The bus station was almost deserted by the time I arrived, and the booking clerk hardly gave me a glance as he spun a ticket towards me and change tinkled into the dish.

"Next bus ain't till five-thirty, mister," he said flatly. "There's a coffee machine over to the news-stand. Best we can do this time of night."

I thanked him and moved off across the compound. He didn't seem to have noticed that I had one hand concealed inside my coat.

My training in the local dialect certainly would not have given cause for suspicion. The last thing I wanted was some promotion-happy cop nosing around before I arrived at my destination.

Things weren't really all that different here from the way they were back home, although the language was, perhaps, a little more colloquial. Mustn't forget that. Could give the game away.

The phrase book they'd provided was committed to memory. Some of the contents were unlikely ever to be required but, by extended literal translation, they might still be useful. It seemed that, in order to avoid electrocution by static discharge during inclement weather, it is advisable to locate oneself at some distance from the nearest postillion. It should also be immediately possible to recognise a grandmother since this individual would be carrying an umbrella held together with string.

Footsteps echoed across the station yard. A uniformed individual plonked a black metal box onto a bench and sat beside it. He produced a girlie magazine from an inside pocket and opened out the centrefold. He must have noticed me studying him because he suddenly turned the open page towards me.

"You got some kinda problem with this, mister?"

I did, but nothing that would have made any sense to him. He muttered something about 'damned faggot'. Not a phrase that I was familiar with, so I said nothing and his attention returned to the magazine.

I fed a coin into the slot on the newsstand and opened the lid, only to be immediately reminded of the danger of my mission.

"BLAZING AIRCRAFT DESTROYS MILITARY BASE."

The report beneath the banner headline continued: 'The pilot of the aircraft which crashed into a military base in the early hours of this morning is believed to have mistaken the lights of the base for a landing strip. A spokesman at the base has assured us that there were no other casualties and that no further statement would be made in the interests of national security.

'The as-yet-unidentified aircraft was first spotted by a motorist who told our reporter that it appeared to be on fire from nose to tail. He thought that it was an unusually large shooting star or a comet but, then, as it turned and headed straight for the base, he realised that it was under some kind of control.'

Just like the Press. No different from our own back home. Full of hypotheses and unsupported speculation. At least nobody had suggested that it was deliberate. But then, they did say that the pilot was destroyed with his aircraft. Nobody, then, would be looking for me.

Tuneless whistling broke into my thoughts.

"Mornin', Harry."

The whistler greeted the man with the girlie magazine.

"Nearly didn't make it. That there big bang sure stirred up a whole heap of crackpots. Been watching the newscast. And they still ain't caught up with that there bank robber yet...

Harry looked up.

"Yeah? What kinda crackpots?"

"Oh. just about the lot, I guess. Every kinda nut in the book from fairies to flyin' saucers and Retributionists."

He took a steaming cup out of the coffee machine.

"Some guy had some cockamamie notion that it was a giant firefly. Got hisself so worked up they had to cart him off to the funny farm."

Smiling at the thought, I sat on a hard bench and tuned in again to the conversation.

It was Harry's turn to speculate.

"No mention of sabotage? Seems to me that'd be a prime target..."

The roar of an incoming bus drowned him out.

Boarding the bus, I took a seat at the back from where I should be able to study the other passengers. Only two seats were occupied: one by an obviously newly-wed couple, the other by a large, uncomfortable-looking man in an ill-fitting grey suit. He raised a curious eyebrow as I passed then settled down to resume his disturbed sleep. The young couple were too wrapped up in one another to take any notice of me.

After a few minutes wait, the driver clambered aboard, and the bus headed out of the depot and was soon speeding along the desert highway.

The next town came and went. I doubt if the young couple even noticed. The big man grunted and shifted his position.

Another hour passed, then a soft buzzing from the big man's wrist jogged him into bleary-eyed consciousness. He stood unsteadily and reached up to the rack above his head just as the bus swung round a bend into the main street of another town, sending him off balance. The heavy case hit the floor and burst open, spilling banknotes into the gangway.

The young man was suddenly awake.

"Holy Cow!" He unwound himself from his companion and leaned down towards the crisp bundles. "Here, let me..."

The offer was cut short by the big man.

"You just let it be, right where it is."

There was a short-barreled gun in his hand.

"Now, both of you get down to the back seat! Pronto!"

He motioned threateningly with the gun.

As the couple joined me at one end of the gangway, the big man backed towards the other. Reaching the front of the bus, he held the gun at the astonished driver's temple.

"Just keep going," he growled, "and nobody's going to get hurt."

We left the town far behind and had covered several miles when the flashing lights of a police road block could be seen up ahead. As the driver braked, the gunman, who had been facing back along the bus, looked over his shoulder and let out an oath.

Heavily armed police surrounded the bus almost before it had stopped.

"Okay. Everybody out!" A bull-horn sounded from outside. "And keep your hands in the air where we can see 'em."

The gunman crouched down, concealing himself from the police. He signaled to the young couple and me to go forward until we stood in the doorway. I felt the gun pressing into the middle of my back.

"Right, you! Don't try any tricks. Okay, now... out."

We did as we were told, our hands high in the air. The big man followed, gun in one hand and the proceeds of his crime in the other.

Hardly had his feet reached the dusty roadway than I turned, slid my concealed hand from under my coat and gently relieved him of the gun.

His jaw opened and closed in silent disbelief as the gun vanished beneath my coat. Tears welled up in his astonished eyes and he looked as though he might succumb to hysteria.

I took him firmly by the arm and led him towards the waiting police. Handcuffs were snapped onto his wrists and he was bundled swiftly away. The chief turned his attention to me.

"How the hell did you do that with both

hands above your head?" He held out his hand. "Oh, and I'll take the gun..."

"I'm afraid I made rather a mess of your military base, officer," I explained. "My craft was programmed to destroy all such installations."

He looked puzzled.

"The gun?" he persisted, snapping his fingers.

My mind raced through the phrase book for the traditional greeting.

I slid the gun out of my coat and held it out towards him, butt first.

He stared hysterically at my middle hand with its central thumb.

"I come in peace and unarmed," I recited. "I extend to your world the Hand of Friendship. Take me to your leader." ◆

Rust

The great yellow wall appeared out of nowhere.

Philip reacted instinctively and spun the wheel, slewing his car across the road.

The wheels had barely stopped when a steel-helmeted head was thrust in through the open window of the car.

"What the hell d'you think you're playing at?" He was almost deafened by the shout. "You want to look where you're going, mate. Weighs twenty tons does that."

The ganger waved an arm towards the giant earthmover that towered above them, rocking on its great wheels and snorting black diesel smoke into the winter air.

"You could wreck a tower-block with that kiddie. It'd have your car for breakfast."

Philip looked sheepish.

"Sorry. Didn't see the lights change."

He shoved the gear lever into reverse and manoeuvred the car back beyond the traffic signal.

As the huge machine rumbled drunkenly away across the muddy desert of embryonic motorway, the lights changed to green and Philip resumed his journey.

That was a close thing. A couple more seconds and...

He shuddered.

Typical of local government, he thought sourly. All the searches had been carried out most thoroughly when he had bought the cottage. Not a sniff of a motorway then.

A lot had happened in that two years. No, less than that, in fact. Somebody must have known something. You can't just go round carving up the countryside at a moment's notice.

Of course, the value of the cottage had plummeted.

The estate agent hadn't been much help either.

"No, not with the motorway coming that close, Mr South. There's the vibration, you see. And the dust. No. I don't really think you'd find anyone would be interested. Now, if it had been a couple of hundred yards nearer... The other side of the river, say... you'd have had no access at all. Then you might have had a case for compensation. Sorry, but there it is."

And there it was. A most expensive white elephant, miles from anywhere. That had been its attraction. An ideal location for a writer. Situated about a mile from the main road, on a bend in the broad lane that led up to the disused quarry, it had been perfect. Perfect, that is, until Amanda had become bored.

Then the rows had started. Philip had been

forced to lock himself in his office to get away from the endless bickering from the time they got up, right into the small hours. Eventually, Amanda had taken to her bed. Romance, if that was what it had been, had long since shed its leaves.

By the time he pulled into the car park beside a modern apartment block, Philip no longer felt guilty at the thought of deceiving Amanda. Jessica, as warm when they were together as Amanda had once been, had always made her feelings perfectly clear. He was sure that he could rely on her for support. He stepped out of the lift and let himself into the smartly furnished apartment. As the door closed behind him, Jessica came out of the bathroom knotting a towel around her wet hair. Philip took in the smile of welcome and the revealing drape of her bathrobe.

In that single moment, he knew that Amanda would have to die.

"There is a way," he said later as he sat on the edge of the bed and adjusted his tie. He bit down on the inside of one cheek, waiting for Jessica's reaction.

"I thought you said she wouldn't divorce you."

Jessica pulled the sheet up around her chin.

"I wasn't thinking of divorce." Philip almost spat out the words. "There's more than one way to..."

"Kill the cat? Oh, it's not very nice to call her a cat, darling."

Jessica looked coy.

"Look, I didn't mean..."

"Didn't you, darling." The sheet fell revealingly away. "Aren't I worth it?"

Philip forced himself to turn away. He picked up his jacket. They had never spoken like this before. There had been a sudden, dramatic shift in their relationship. It could never be the same again.

There was a rustle from behind him then Jessica's arms were around him and he could feel her warmth of her nakedness against his back.

"You didn't answer my question."

"I shall need your help."

The warmth withdrew as Jessica sat back onto the bed and hugged the sheet around her.

"Oh, no. I'm not getting involved. If you're really serious, then all right. You go ahead. But I don't want to know the details."

"Okay. No details. But, if everything goes according to plan, I'll get rid of the cottage and I'll end up with quite a bit from the insurance."

Suddenly Jessica was interested.

"How?"

"Well," Philip lowered his voice. "Amanda's life is insured. So is the cottage. Now if the cottage were to collapse while she was under the influence of those sleeping pills of hers..."

"You'd collect the lot." There was greed in Jessica's green eyes at the thought. "So? How are you going to arrange it?"

"By pulling it down."

Philip's matter-of-fact tone made Jessica explode into laughter.

"You know you really had me fooled for a moment. I thought you were serious..."

"I'm deadly serious. If you'd just shut up a minute and listen."

Philip could feel anger beginning to rise.

"It was that incident this morning that gave me the idea. I'm going to borrow one of those earthmovers. They don't call them that for nothing. Even from a quarter of a mile away, they shake the cottage to its foundations. It's one of the reasons that I can't sell the place. When the quarry was closed, a lot of rusty old cables and things were left there. If I attach them to the cottage, I can easily pull it down."

"But what about the cables and tyre marks all over the place?"

Philip's chest swelled visibly.

"There won't be any. I won't have to take the machine within a hundred yards of the cottage. There's more than enough cable to reach that far. Afterwards, I can untangle it and throw it into the river. Then I return the machine to where I got it from and, by morning, no-one will know it's been moved."

"It might just work, at that." Jessica thought for a moment. "But how will you explain your not being in the cottage when it happens?"

"That's where you come in. I shall be here with you."

"You... you... what?" Jessica was horrified. "You must be out of your mind. If that doesn't involve me, nothing will."

"Look, if I choose to be unfaithful to my wife, that doesn't mean that I'd necessarily want to kill her. But it does give me the perfect alibi. What's more, there would be no reason to stop seeing each other. I could hardly be expected to mourn for a woman I was being unfaithful to."

There was a short silence. Philip felt a little uneasy as Jessica studied him coldly.

"When are you going to do it then?"

"Tomorrow night about midnight. You can expect me any time after about half-past three."

It was close to one o'clock by the time Philip had carried the cables up the narrow path from the quarry floor and attached them to the old stonework. He drove down to the main road and parked in the entrance to a field some distance from the road works. It was dark and there were icy patches underfoot as he stumbled towards the place where all the earthmovers were parked for the night. The first he saw of them was a gigantic silhouette against the moonless sky. Making his way up to the cab, he produced a pencil torch from his pocket and, shielding the beam carefully, he examined the controls.

After a few minutes, he started up the engine and switched on the headlights.

The clutch came up with a jolt and it was too late to turn back.

Swiftly gaining confidence, he straightened the vehicle to cross the bridge. The steering shifted in his hands and the headlights reflected sullenly on the swollen waters.

Suddenly, there was a shriek of tearing metal and rusty girders buckling under immense weight.

The dull grey dawn picked out the side of a single gigantic tyre, jutting from the icy water like a small island.

Suspended above it from the twisted remains of the bridge, a broken sign swung slowly in the cold morning air.

'Unsuitable for Heavy Vehicles.' ◆

Once Bitten...

"I think you'll want to see this patient personally, Doctor."

I looked up from my desk at the sound of the nurse's voice.

"Why? What's special about this one?" I asked. We get all kinds in Casualty at half past two in the morning.

"Cubicle Three. Says he's been bitten by a vampire."

I must have looked surprised. The nurse smiled, lifting her head slightly to one side and stroking the base of her neck with one finger, drawing my attention to the pale, soft flesh there before moving on and tapping her temple.

The message was clear. I gave a wry smile and picked up my stethoscope.

The patient was sitting on the bed, holding a handkerchief to his neck. I introduced myself and examined the wound.

"What kind of vampire was it?" I asked casually. "I mean... bat... the Undead? You're sure it wasn't a snake, are you? It's easy to make a mistake when you've just been bitten by something a bit... er... unusual, shall we say?"

The man leapt to his feet.

"OK. Laugh all you want, but I've been

studying and writing about vampires for the last twenty-odd years and I know what I'm talking about."

He started to leave.

I held up a hand. "Hold on a moment, Mr… er…?"

"Pentecost. Jason Pentecost."

He sat down again.

"First of all, I'm not saying that I don't believe you. I'm simply saying that you could be mistaken. I have to know all the facts before I can be of any help. Now, you're sure that it wasn't a snake?"

"It'd have to be a damned big snake to have fangs this far apart. I'd have been dead long before now." He uncovered the wound again to prove his point.

I had to agree.

"Anyway, the vampire bat isn't native to these shores. It has very small fangs and usually bites its victim on the big toe during sleep." I wondered if I was beginning to sound a bit flippant. If so, he didn't seem to have noticed.

"Which brings us to the third possibility—the Undead. That's a bit unusual in these parts, so I think you'd better tell me the whole story."

Pentecost flexed his neck as though stiffness was beginning to set in.

"I met a girl at a club earlier this evening. We had a few drinks, we danced for a while, had dinner and went back to my place. Maja—that was her name—had it all and we ended up in bed together.

"It was absolute bliss. I'd never met anyone like her.

"Well, I was totally exhausted after that, so we lay there together for a while and I dozed off.

"I was faintly aware of her bending over me and felt her kiss me long and deeply on my neck. I just lay there, enjoying the sensation. When I finally opened my eyes, she was gone. Of course, I wanted to see her again so I started to dress to go after her."

He swallowed hard.

"That's when I found the wound on my neck."

I tried hard to adjust the scepticism in my reply.

"Forgive me asking, Mr Pentecost, but if this is your field of expertise—just being curious, you understand—wouldn't you carry some kind of safeguard? Garlic... or... a crucifix... or something?"

With his free hand he took a clove of garlic out of his pocket and dropped it onto the bed.

"Millions of people hate garlic. You probably know someone who does. I know several. That doesn't make them vampires. It's all part of the legend. And as for crucifixes, vampires have nothing to do with religion."

"They're not that much different from us." He went on. "They can even survive sunlight."

I picked up one of the garlic cloves and savoured its aroma.

"So, what happens now?"

"I'll be ready next time."

I raised an eyebrow. "What makes you think there'll be a next time?"

"She has to finish the job so that I'll become one of the Undead."

I tried not to smirk. "What are you going to do? Shoot her?"

He took in a deep breath and let it out sharply.

"That's the one thing the legends are right about. Ordinary bullets can't hurt them. But silver bullets can. Well, it's the silver really. If the slightest trace gets into their bloodstream, it's fatal. It reacts with their enzymes. The funny thing is, it's the same enzymes in their saliva that turn their victims into new vampires. But the bite has to be fatal for it to work. That's how I know that she'll be back. She has to come back to complete the job. My gun is always ready under my pillow. If I'd realised what Maja was, I'd have used it before. But, as the old saying goes, 'once bitten...'

"And what if she doesn't come back?"

"I'll track her and the rest of her kind down and wipe them out. Every last one of them."

He seemed quite detached about what I would have considered to be a massacre, but I let him have his fantasy and returned to the job in hand.

"I'd better cauterise that wound to stop the bleeding." I said and saw his expression change. "It's OK, this is not the Middle Ages. Things have progressed quite a bit since then. We don't use red-hot irons nowadays. We use chemicals. It's quite painless."

He relaxed visibly, and it took only minutes to complete the procedure. I dressed the wound, bid him 'good hunting' then I went back to my office and dialled home.

"I cauterised the wound with silver nitrate. You were quite right, Maja. He knew far too much about us. His blood's so full of your enzymes that he'll be dead before dawn." ◆

Vital Signs

Paula was vaguely aware of flashing lights and the smell of petrol. The intense pain that had flushed through her whole being, had retreated into a warm knot in the small of her back.

Through closed eyelids, she could sense the purposeful movements of people around her. Kind words and crisp instructions mingled, reassuring her that she was in good hands and that she would soon be released.

A hand rested gently on her forehead and she felt her eyelids being opened. A shaft of light shone once... twice... again. Then the other eye.

The hand was removed, and the light vanished. She heard a man's voice close to her face. His words, almost meaningless, conjured disjointed pictures in her head.

School children... Taking no notice...

"Just like children..." she thought.

No! That was wrong!

Pupils... Not responding...

That was it. Not children.

The suggestion of children tugged at her muddled thoughts.

Jenny!

Dear God!

Not today!

Not like this!

"Posie." Paula felt the faint touch of lips on her cheek as the word was whispered into her ear. "It's all right, Posie. I'm here. I won't leave you."

She could smell the apple scent of the long red hair that fell across her face. She wanted to shout out "Jenny, is that you?" and hold her close again. She tried to open her eyes as firm hands tore at the front of her blouse and something cold was pressed against her chest.

"She's arrested!"

The blouse was ripped open and she felt the pressure of hard metal on her left side and another between her breasts. There was a high-pitched whine.

"Clear..."

As the warning was delivered, she was convulsed by indescribable pain.

"Don't be afraid, Posie. I'm still with you..."

The quiet voice eased the pain and Paula was aware of being moved.

The night air breathed cold against her skin, and a blanket was wrapped around her. She felt herself being lifted on a stretcher. Doors closed at her feet and a siren blared into the darkness. An engine, muffled and far away, roared into life and sudden panic clawed its way into Paula's mind as a mask was slipped over her face.

"Jenny. Jenny, don't leave me. Don't let them take me."

Small, cool fingers slid between her own and squeezed reassuringly. The familiar smell of apples filled her senses and the panic ebbed.

Above the siren's wail, a man's voice was raised in one-sided conversation.

"RTA... Junction of Turners Lane and Pitt's Hill... One casualty... Female... Early fifties... Comatose... Possible spinal damage... Have the crash team standing by... ETA zero six minutes..."

Slowly, the meaning began to filter through the surrounding noise.

Paula tried frantically to shout out "I'm not! I'm not in a coma. I can hear. I can feel. Jenny, tell them. Tell them, please."

The grip on her hand tightened, but she was unable to respond, and no sound came. Silk-soft hair trailed across her face and she could feel Jenny's breath warm against her cheek.

"Try not to worry, Posie. We'll soon be there. It'll soon be over, you'll see."

"But I can't see. My eyes. They won't open. I can't move."

"It's all right, Posie. Trust me."

The sirens stopped, and the ambulance doors were thrown open. Paula felt herself being moved out and along. She was conscious of people running alongside, of passing beneath an endless succession of bright lights—and of Jenny's grip on her fingers slipping...

The lights dimmed, and the indescribable pain returned. Then again. And again. A shaft of pure fire burned through her chest and woke her sleeping heart. The pain came again, and hollow voices boomed around her.

"We have a pulse... eighty over sixty and rising... She's back with us... Respiration shallow but steady..."

"Open your eyes, Posie." Small fingers touched her temple.

Paula screwed up her eyes and opened them very slowly. She caught a glimpse of long red hair against the light, then a white-coated figure blotted out the scene and shone a small light into her eyes.

"She's coming out of it. Pupils are responsive, but sluggish. What did you say her name was? Right... Mrs Acott... Paula... You've been in a nasty accident... I'm Doctor Laslett. You're in the County Hospital. You're going to be all right. Can you hear me? Just blink if you can understand what I'm saying..."

"Jenny... Please..." Paula whispered, almost soundlessly.

The doctor's voice came again.

"You mustn't try to talk. You're very weak..."

Paula took no notice.

"Jenny," she repeated. "Let her stay with me. Don't send her away..."

"You really mustn't talk, Mrs Acott. You need all the rest you can get. Now we want you to get some sleep..."

"But she was here..." Paula protested weakly. "I saw her..."

She felt a slight pressure on her arm and dropped away into darkness.

When light returned, it was accompanied by the smell of anti-septic and the soft, regular beeping of a heart monitor. Behind a large window that occupied most of one wall of the small ward, the doctor who had spoken to her earlier was in conversation with a blue-uniformed ward sister. Grey daylight, venturing between half drawn curtains, brightened as though heavy clouds had suddenly parted. A reflection in the glass made Paula gasp as the sunlight threw into sharp relief a figure standing half hidden by a tent-like structure that held the bedclothes away from her legs.

"Jenny... Oh, Jenny..."

Paula's heart beat faster and the quiet beep became irregular.

Within moments, the room was filled with blue and white. Voices passed back and forth, and the beep settled back into its steady rhythm. The sister made an adjustment to the bed, propping Paula up into a more comfortable position.

"I'm afraid we haven't been able to contact your daughter yet," she said quietly. "Is there anyone else we can get in touch with, Mrs Acott? Your husband, perhaps?"

Paula felt for the gold ring she wore on her left hand. It was not there.

"It's all right, dear..." The sister patted Paula's hands reassuringly. "It's in your handbag. We took it off when you were first brought in. You can put it on again now. If you'd like..."

Taking Paula's handbag out of a bedside cabinet, she produced the ring and slipped it gently onto Paula's finger.

"There we are, Mrs Acott..." She snapped the handbag shout.

"No... no... it's our mother's ring. It's a bit loose..." Paula put her hand up to her neck. "Where's my locket?"

Her voice faltered with the effort. "I never take it off... Please..."

"Yes, of course." The sister opened the bag again and took out the locket. It was open. "Oh, how pretty. You must be very proud of them. And they'll be twins, of course. They're so alike with that long red hair. Such pretty names, too. Jenny and... Posie, is it?"

Paula smiled as the sister fastened the gold chain around her neck.

Paula held up the open locket. "Jenny is my twin. It's our birthday. She's called me Posie ever since she could first talk. There was an accident. We were twelve. Jenny... never got any older. I've had to grow older for both of us. She was here. She won't be far away. She'll be back soon. She promised..."

The locket slid from Paula's fingers. The monitor's rhythm faltered and became a steady tone.

Unaware of the urgent movement around her, Paula lay still, her gaze fixed on the small figure waiting with outstretched arms in a beautiful orchard just beyond the foot of the bed. ◆

Fast Forward

DI Glover stared at the small, balding man across the desk.

"You can't possibly expect me to believe this?"

His tone was flat, and the question pointed. His visitor shrugged.

"Whether you believe it or not, Detective Inspector, is irrelevant."

"All right then, Mr Cooper. Let's just go over it again."

Glover took a notebook from his desk drawer. Clicking a ball pen into life, he opened the book and dated the first page.

"Let's start at the part that says that I'm going to be arrested for your murder." A wry smile flickered at the corner of his mouth. "Until you walked into my office with this fantastic story, I'd never laid eyes on you, so why would I want to kill you?"

The response was timid, almost apologetic.

"Oh, let's say it's just the way things turned out."

"Ah!" The detective slapped the desk. "You said 'the way things turned out'. I noticed that you keep using the past tense. If I did intend to kill you—which, I assure you, I don't—it hasn't happened yet, so why the past tense?"

"Because it has happened, Inspector. Time

just hasn't caught up with it yet, that's all. Oh, dear!" Cooper sighed and looked up at the clock over the office door. "I knew that this would be difficult. Look. It's nearly twenty past three. Let me prove it to you."

He slid a hand inside his raincoat and took out a plastic case from which he produced a video disc.

"I know you have a machine that will play this. Would you put it on, please? Humour me…"

Sliding open a cupboard to reveal a DVD recorder and television set, the detective inserted the disc and touched a button. Instantly, the screen was illuminated by familiar race-track scenes with a tightly bunched field of horses crossing the line. He turned up the volume just in time to hear the excited tones of the commentator ring out.

"… with Flemish Bond in third place. Wedgwood Lad has won the Thrasted Handicap at sixteen to one—the first time in the history of this great race that a rank outsider has even made it into the first three…"

He turned the sound down again.

"Look. If this is some kind of joke…" he began.

"No, Inspector. It's no joke." Cooper cut in. "I've been here in your office now for… what?

Twenty minutes, give or take? Will you just rewind it and look at it again."

Puzzled, Glover did so. The same scene, the same commentary. Before he was able to question the significance, Cooper produced a newspaper from his pocket and spread it out across the desk.

"Would you now turn off the video and switch over to the television. Er... Channel Three, if you wouldn't mind..."

Glover complied and switched through the channels. A black and white film, a children's programme—and a race meeting identical to the one that he had just seen. He turned up the volume.

"And, as they reach the line, it's Wedgwood Lad by a neck from Tyrell's Loch with Flemish Bond in third place. Wedgwood Lad has won the Thrasted Handicap at sixteen to one—the first time in the history of this great race that a rank outsider has even made it into the first three..."

Glover turned down the commentator's excited tones and stared in amazement at Cooper.

"That's impossible! How the hell could you have recorded a race that hadn't yet been run?"

Cooper spread the newspaper on the desk and pointed to the TV coverage of the Thrasted Handicap, starting at ten past three.

"I told you, Inspector. Time hasn't caught up yet. But it will..." He indicated the football fixtures for the following Saturday. "I can show you the results of every one of these matches..." He tailed off, amused by the detective's puzzled expression.

"But...?" It took Glover a few seconds to drag his mind away from the lucrative possibilities that were concealed in that simple, matter-of-fact statement. "I still don't see what all this has to do with me. There's no crime involved." Then he added: "Unless the wrong type of people get hold of this."

"You've heard the expression 'Que sera, sera', have you not, Inspector? 'What will be, will be'?"

The policeman nodded dumbly.

"Well, it works the other way around, too," Cooper went on. "I'm sure you would agree that 'what has been, has been'." He held out the newspaper, pointing to several small items. "Fillers," he said. "Hardly news at all. They wouldn't get on television. But world events, sports, strikes, crime waves and the like. Those are news. They get on television. And, if they get on television, they can be recorded. Right?"

Another nod.

"Well, I dabble in electronics, Inspector. I've modified my video equipment to record events that are *going* to be broadcast."

Grover found his tongue. "But they all do that..."

Cooper shook his head, slowly.

"Not quite. They can only record a broadcast as it happens. You set the timer to switch on when the broadcast is transmitted, and Bob's your uncle. I can do the same thing, but without waiting for the broadcast to take place..."

Something seemed to click in Glover's brain.

"But that means that you could prevent something from happening because you know about it before the event."

Cooper shrugged.

"Unfortunately, it doesn't work like that. Look at it this way. An event can only be broadcast as it happens or after it has taken place. My machine records the broadcast of the event, not the event itself. Now, since I can record that broadcast before it is transmitted, it follows that the event must take place or else there would be no broadcast to record. Right?"

Glover nodded.

"Sounds logical. In an illogical sort of way, I suppose. What else have you... er... recorded?" He turned back to the machine and reached for the controls.

"There's a blank bit in a moment, explained

Cooper, "then the sports results for next Saturday, followed by the News. If you whiz it through, there's something there that will interest you."

Glover held down the fast-forward button. As the screen filled with the following Saturday's full-time football results, he could appreciate the effect that such a machine would have on the betting world. The News followed at break-neck speed, until Glover realised that a familiar figure was being interviewed by a reporter. He rewound to the beginning of the item. It concerned the body of a woman, discovered in a wooded area about two miles from her home.

"Police are withholding the identity of the woman, believed to be in her middle thirties, until the next of kin have been informed."

The reporter turned to the tall man beside him.

"Detective Inspector Glover is the officer in charge of the investigation," he continued. "I understand that the woman's handbag was found close to the body, Inspector. So, presumably, you've been able to make a positive identification?"

Glover watched in astonishment as his screen image nodded and looked directly into the camera.

"Yes," he said. "We are fairly certain that we

know the identity of the victim, but as to the motive or the identity of her killer... well... I can assure members of the public that everything that can be done to bring this criminal to justice will be done. We have a number of leads to go on and expect to make an arrest within the next twenty-four hours."

The reporter signed off and returned the programme to the studio.

Glover turned off the machine and, hardly daring to believe what he had just seen, sat back in silence as the seconds ticked away.

"How could I be so sure of an arrest?" he said, eventually. "How could anyone? Even a confession isn't absolute proof."

The small man stood up, giving him a knowing look as he reached across to take the disc out of the machine.

"You could be there when the murder takes place. You can't stop it happening, but you know when and where it's going to happen. I should take a good camera if I were you."

Before the full implication of the suggestion could sink in, the small man had left the office.

Concealed among the bushes, not ten yards from the spot where the murder was to take place, Glover heard muffled cries for help but could see nothing. There had been no mention on the video of the thick overnight fog that had rendered the camera useless. Knowing that he could do nothing to prevent the crime, he tried desperately to identify the killer. Suddenly, he found himself grappling with the villain. Then, like a weapon, the woman's body was thrust at him, bowling him over as the killer vanished into the fog.

Winded, he lay for a moment looking up at the sky. The fog was thick at ground level but not deep. A full moon illuminated the upper layers with an eerie glow. He turned his head towards the dead woman. She lay face-down, her features hidden by a curtain of dark hair. Glover got up and gently rolled her over. Taking out a small torch, he shone it on her face and brushed the hair aside.

The torch clicked off. Glover sank back onto his heels. He had seen too much. Now, he could see nothing. His normally unemotional facade crumbled in the darkness.

Damn Cooper to Hell!

Why couldn't he have taken his fantastic story to some other station?

Tears burned his eyes with the knowledge that his two-year affair with Margaret Bailey had reached an abrupt and dreadful end.

He had grappled with her killer—and had let him escape. He knew that there was no way to explain the night's events to anyone. Who would believe such a story? Where was the proof?

By the time the television interview took place, Glover had a plan. He would personally inform Margaret's husband, of whom she had only ever spoken on the occasion of their first meeting. He could then find out whether her infidelity had been suspected and, if so, to what extent. He would then call on Cooper, get him to record the broadcast in which the name of the killer was to be announced. Then, based on that knowledge, he would use normal procedures to find the evidence that would lead to certain arrest. He knew, now, why he'd sounded so confident during the interview.

Finding no response to the front doorbell, Glover let himself into the house with Margaret's own key taken from her handbag after the forensic experts had pronounced it clean. As the door clicked shut behind him, a feint whirring made him look up – straight into the Cyclopean eye of a closed-circuit television camera.

"Do come in, Inspector." It was Cooper's voice. "Don't look so surprised. You really shouldn't be, you know. I had to give a false name and address in order to get you here. I'm in the lounge. Won't you come in? It's a little strange when I can see you, but you can't see me. Almost like a children's game."

Glover found the lounge door slightly ajar.

He pushed it wide open and surveyed the room. The man he knew as Cooper was sitting in an armchair with his back to the door, watching the picture from the camera on a monitor screen in the far corner of the room. It showed a back view of Glover, framed in the doorway.

"You've probably already guessed as much, Inspector, but let me introduce myself properly. George Bailey, husband – or should I say widower – of the late Margaret Bailey. I had to kill her, you know. She was being unfaithful to me. But, of course, you already know that."

He touched a button on a control unit beside the chair. The picture on the monitor changed to a view of Glover from another camera inside the room.

"As you can see, Inspector, everything that happens here will receive all the news coverage it deserves. Every move you make is being recorded direct from these cameras."

He touched another switch. A new picture appeared on the screen.

"See for yourself, Inspector. I sent an edited copy of this video to my solicitor, to be played in the event of my death."

The screen showed a struggle between the two men, culminating in Glover striking the small man on the head with a heavy object just as the screen went blank. That it would be incriminating was beyond doubt. Taken from a high viewpoint, the scene gave prominence to the finality of the blow and clearly identified both men.

"If the signal is taken directly from the camera, it doesn't have to be broadcast, but it can still be recorded in the same way. As I'm sure you've realised by now, there's nothing you can do to prevent it."

Glover knew that the smug, self-satisfied tone was meant to goad him into some kind of response. He could see no way to prevent the scene that he had just witnessed from happening.

"We'll see about that"

In desperation he leaned across the back of the armchair and grabbed the control box. It was fairly heavy but had no wires to hold it down. He turned to leave the room, but the small man leapt up and tried to snatch the unit back.

Somehow, Glover managed to retain his grip on the object as they struggled. He felt anger rising. He remembered Margaret's body lying up there on the damp ground. He was beginning to believe that he wanted to kill this man.

Wielding the control box above his head, he brought it down with all his strength. There was a searing pain in his hand and the control box shattered in a shower of sparks as it glanced off the corner of a low marble coffee table and struck the small man across the temple.

Glover's anger subsided as his hand grew numb. He lay for several minutes regaining his breath and was relieved to see that the other man was still breathing. Kneeling up, he rolled the unconscious man over with his good hand and snapped handcuffs onto his wrists.

"You overlooked one very important point," he explained when Cooper regained consciousness. "Your machine, however ingenious it might be, could not record an event that would take place after the machine itself had ceased to function. You assumed that the blow you received would kill you and that the evidence you sent to your solicitor would be conclusive. But the control box was hidden from the camera when it was broken."

He paused to let it sink in.

"No, my friend, if you had tried to look ahead to what the cameras are seeing now, you would have seen nothing. It was the control box that made your invention work. Without it, the recorder is just like any other. And the unedited evidence that's inside it has your full confession on it." ♦

Cause of Death

Doc Williams finished sharpening his pencil and was about to return to his crossword when a squeal of skidding tyres sounded outside the bar. A moment later, a young man rushed in from the street and shouted excitedly to the bartender.

"Hey, Mac! Better call a doctor. There's a guy been hurt..."

The bartender, squinted up at the light through the glass that he was polishing. Disgruntled at being called 'Mac' but otherwise unmoved by the other's sense of urgency, he breathed on the glass and grunted annoyance.

"You wanna doctor... you gotta doctor," he growled.

He nodded towards the stubble-jawed figure at the other end of the bar.

"Name's Williams..."

The young man summed Doc up in a flash.

"What? That barfly? Okay, so you're a funny man."

Doc, swaying a little, took a deep breath and started towards the door.

"It's okay, son," he mumbled. "I'm licensed."

Despite the late hour, by the time Doc reached the scene of the accident a sizeable crowd had gathered. He pushed his way through and knelt beside the injured man who lay motionless, half hidden under the front of a truck.

His flesh was pallid in the glare of car headlights, and his breathing was scarcely perceptible. Doc gently lifted the man's wrist. No pulse.

With an almost forgotten skill, Doc examined the man quickly but thoroughly before deciding that no harm would be done by moving him. Satisfied, he rolled the inert form onto one side. Apart from a fair-sized cut on one temple, there seemed to be no apparent injury. Doc shuddered at the unnatural appearance of the cut. Instantly the remnants of his semi-permanent hangover were gone. There was no blood, no contusion.

Only once had Doc ever seen cut like that. He looked closely at the man's face. It was the face that had haunted him for nearly two years. Nobody would have believed him then. There had been no point in trying to explain. Why should anyone believe him now?

Doc knew that he had to act quickly. But what to do?

He thought back to the night that Mrs Lumley had died. On that occasion he had been unprepared...

"Calling Doctor Williams; Doctor Williams,

please."

In response to the treacly voice that oozed from the loudspeaker, Doc picked up the nearest telephone.

"Oh, Doctor, Mrs Lumley, Room 746. Her son just called in. He'll be along in the morning to take her home. She says will you go in and see her before you check out."

"Sure. I'll look in later. You just caught me on the way to the theatre. Tell her not to worry. I'll be along."

As usual, Doc's duties in the Emergency Department kept him busy late into the night. When, eventually, he remembered his promise, it was almost midnight. Since his route took him right past Mrs Lumley's room, he paused at her door and looked at his watch.

"No," he thought. "She needs all the rest she can get."

He smiled and decided to see her first thing in the morning.

As he turned to go, there was a sound of movement from inside the room. It was as though something had been knocked over—then caught before it had reached the floor.

The corridor lights streamed in as Doc opened the door.

From a half-crouching position, a pale, dark-haired man spun towards him, his teeth bared in a canine snarl. A tumbler, clenched in one hand, shattered as the grip tightened, causing shards of glass to cut deep into the flesh. Then the man was across the room, slamming Doc back against the wall with his injured hand in his haste to get away.

Collecting his scattered wits, Doc's first concern was for his patient.

The man wouldn't get far with that hand.

Mrs Lumley's face wore a look of terror, frozen into the pallor of death. By the time the autopsy was performed there was nothing to indicate the cause of death. The coroner's verdict of 'Death due to heart failure, following a severe traumatic experience' was at least consistent with the physical evidence. No actual blame was laid, but the inference was drawn that Mrs Lumley had been awakened by the tumbler smashing on the floor. Seeing Doc standing over her, the shock had proven too much for her already weak heart.

The following day, banner headlines declared: 'DOCTOR SCARES WOMAN TO DEATH'. The Press, in their usual unending quest for sensationalism, had pronounced sentence.

Mrs Lumley's son could not prove negligence on the part of Doc, nor of the hospital. But, when private patients began taking their business elsewhere, Doc's resignation was firmly requested.

Over the weeks that followed, Doc tried hard to persuade himself that he had been right not to mention the real cause of death. At night he would wake up sweating, haunted by that face. His days were spent searching for some sign of the killer.

Gradually, the long days and sleepless nights coalesced into a soothing alcoholic fog, just thick enough to keep the memories at bay. One day it might all blow over. Meanwhile...

Doc rolled the injured man onto his back. He felt revulsion for this... this... creature. Just to touch the cold flesh made him want to throw up.

The cut on the man's temple was already beginning to heal over.

Bending low over the still figure, Doc placed one hand over the other, pressing sharply, regularly over the sternum.

"He's doing a heart massage," came a know-it-all voice from the crowd.

A low murmur bubbled from the thin lips. The cut had healed completely.

"Well, you did your best, doctor."

The paramedic closed the ambulance doors, concealing the sheet-covered body from view.

"Ain't it just the way, though? A guy gets hit

by a truck and he don't get too badly hurt. Who'd have thought that a pencil from an inside pocket could have pierced his heart like that. I mean, if it had bled some, it might have been easier to find."

Doc stood for a moment as the lights of the wailing ambulance disappeared along the street into the jungle of neon signs.

Doc started to stroll homewards.

"Yes, very strange," he thought wryly, carefully massaging away the small hexagonal indentations in the butt of one hand. "Like the night he pushed me with his cut hand. There was no blood on my theatre gown, either. The cuts had healed over. Just like the two little holes in Mrs Lumley's neck. Maybe, when they do the autopsy, they'll understand."

He shuddered.

"The only people in this world who don't bleed are the dead. And the undead!" ♦

Legacy of Evil

In the blackness, the air escaped from the deflating dinghy like a gigantic death rattle.

Craig rolled a large pack out of the craft. It scrunched on the shingle. He grinned invisibly. His watch glowed 2:43. The bomb would have gone off hours ago. A perfect plan, perfectly executed.

Craig found his torch and was blinded by the explosion of light in the moonless night.

"Better watch that," he thought aloud, thumbing the switch.

Carefully shielding the torch, he switched on again. A quick sweep of the fragmented beam showed the general lay of the beach, then it was dark again.

The dinghy was too big to wedge between the rocks.. After six hours in the damned thing, Craig enjoyed taking a knife to it and was soon perspiring freely despite the chill night air. When it was thoroughly hidden, he turned his attention to more pressing matters.

His stomach rumbled as though he hadn't eaten for days. He struggled with the pack until his groping hands found what he wanted.

"Best not use the torch again until I get farther inland... Damn!"

The jagged lid of the tin ripped painfully across his knuckles. His curse muttered back from the surrounding rocks, accentuating the isolation of the headland. He licked the wound.

"Damn fool situation," he thought. "Stuck on a godforsaken beach without a fire..."

His vacuum flask grated ominously as he started to unscrew the top.

In frustration, he hurled it towards the sound of the invisible breakers. Not even a warming cup of coffee now. He ate the cold baked beans noisily, without interest or enthusiasm.

Setting up a small bivouac in the darkness did nothing to lessen his anger. At least, he thought, he was alive.

Unlike Willis.

Craig smiled at the memory. Willis slumped in the cabin of the plane, the controls moving gently in the phantom grip of the autopilot. The bomb, wedged against the bulkhead, wrapped in all that lovely, useless, incriminating money. He remembered clambering out onto the wing and an eternity of falling before his parachute opened.

Inside the tiny tent, Craig wrapped polythene around the torch and switched on again. After the darkness, the faint glow was more than sufficient. The pack's bulk had been mainly the tent itself and a few cans of food. Tomorrow, he would hitch a lift to the nearest town, and he was home and dry.

He wondered how long it would be before they found Willis and shrugged. They'd think that the plane had blown up in mid-air. And with all that traceable money floating around...

He took a small wash-leather bag out of his anorak pocket and emptied it into his hand. He chuckled. No-one would expect a million quid's worth of diamonds to float. They sparkled in the torchlight. First water, every one. And a buyer already waiting.

Craig stowed the gems safely away, smiled and switched off the torch. Soon, the muffled sound of breakers was in competition with the thunder of hearty snoring.

The sun was already high and the air in the tent was thick when Craig awoke with a raging headache. His throat burned and every muscle ached. His hand was agony and the ragged cut across his knuckles was vividly inflamed.

A narrow track offered the only route off the beach. He reached the top of the rise and collapsed, exhausted. The grass made him sneeze. He sat up and wiped his eyes.

On the beach, close to the remains of his camp, stood a solitary notice board, facing out to sea.

"Do not swim when the red flag is flying," he thought and stood up unsteadily.

Reaching higher ground, Craig's heart

almost stopped. The sea shone in every direction. In the darkness, he had mistaken the island for a headland and, as the mainland taunted him from the horizon, he recalled the pleasure he had derived from destroying the dinghy last night.

Craig had always prided himself on being resourceful. Obviously, there was no way that he could swim that distance in his present condition. However, if the notice board would float, he might paddle it across that distance.

His efforts to dismantle the board proved fruitless and he collapsed on the shingle. Minutes passed. He rolled over and raised himself to his knees, his frustration turning to blinding fear as he saw the warning written on the board.

'Ministry of Defence Property. Anthrax. Do not land.' ♦

Paperweight

Rebecca's eyes were red, and her face was streaked with mascara. She dabbed frantically at her tears in an attempt to hide them as her brother, Larry, came in.

"Hey! What's up, Sis?" he asked, dropping his holdall behind the door. "Has that little weed been upsetting you?"

Rebecca turned away, sobbing.

"Oh, Larry! I do wish you wouldn't call him names. I know you'd prefer me to marry a 'real man', as you put it, but it's not Arnold's fault that he's not big and strong. And, even if he were, he might not want to be a boxer like you anyway."

"Not much chance of that." Larry puffed out his great chest and snorted. "They'd have to put him in a class of his own. 'Paperweight', I shouldn't wonder." He chuckled at the thought. "I can't think what you see in him."

Burying her face in her hands, Rebecca sobbed even harder. Larry's smile faded. Sitting beside her on the sofa, he put his arm around her.

"Hey! C'mon, Sis. I'm sorry. You're really stuck on this guy, aren't you." A sudden anger flashed across his rugged face. "Here, he hasn't... I mean... you're not..."

Rebecca looked up. "Oh, no. Of course not.

Nothing like that. It's just..." She started sobbing again. "I think he's seeing another woman."

Larry's anger changed to brotherly understanding.

"Right, then," he said, kindly. "Why don't you pop upstairs and powder your nose. Then you'd better tell me all about it."

When Rebecca re-joined him, Larry could see why any man would be attracted to her. The tears gone, her soft, round face looked prettily out from its frame of auburn hair. Whatever masculine qualities Arnold might lack, there was little doubt that he had excellent taste in women.

Rebecca settled comfortably in an armchair and took a deep breath.

"I don't really know where to begin," she said. "As you know, I've been going out with Arnold for about four months now. Right at the start, he told me that he works late on Wednesday evenings. I know that the Civil Service expects a certain amount of compulsory overtime, so I've never questioned it."

Rebecca paused.

"Well, as I wasn't seeing him tonight, I went to that Bolshoi Ballet film at the Regal. On the way home, I saw Arnold going into the Kings Arms... with a blonde."

The tears started to well up again.

"Hm-m-m!" Larry looked concerned. "Do you know her? I mean, have you any idea who she is?"

Rebecca sniffed and wiped her eyes.

"Not really. I've seen her around town. It isn't easy to miss her with all the whistles she gets."

"Are you sure he wasn't just holding the door open for her?" Larry couldn't think why he should defend the little weed.

"Of course, I'm sure," Rebecca wept. "They were arm in arm. And besides, Arnold doesn't drink." She leapt up from her chair and ran back upstairs, flinging back over her shoulder, "At least that's what he's always told me."

Larry knew how strongly Rebecca felt about Arnold and only wanted to what was best for her. It would give him great satisfaction to thump the living daylights out of the bloke but that would hurt her even more. Tomorrow, he would find him and warn him off. Better that Rebecca got over her hurt now than to let things go on as they are.

The sound of the garden gate closing broke into his thoughts. Footsteps scrunched up the gravel path and the doorbell chimed.

It was Arnold.

"Sorry it's so late. I don't usually come calling this late. You must be Larry. Mind if I come in? Rebecca's told me so much about you."

Larry ignored the out-stretched hand.

"She's told me about you, too."

He started to close the door, but Arnold ducked under his arm and stepped inside.

Larry grunted. "Weren't you in the King's Arms a few minutes ago?"

Arnold cast his eyes down. "Er...well, yes."

"Smashing bit of stuff you were with. Your sister, was it?"

The question sounded distinctly sour. Arnold looked Larry in the eye.

"No. Just a friend. Look, can I see Rebecca? It's important."

Pulling himself up to his full six-foot-two, the boxer towered over him.

"She... doesn't want to see you," he said firmly, and emphasised every word by prodding Arnold in the chest with one finger.

Arnold removed his glasses and started to polish them on his handkerchief.

"Isn't that for her to decide?"

Damned cheek, thought Larry. At least the little squirt had guts.

"Out!" he snapped, stepping forward with obvious intent.

Arnold dodged Larry's groping hand and turned back to face him.

"Look, enough with the big brother act and

calm down or..."

"Or what? Right. That does it. If you want to get legal..."

Grabbing Arnold by the scruff of his neck, Larry propelled him forcibly towards the door.

"So go ahead! Sue me!"

"No, Larry. Please don't," Rebecca came running down the stairs.

Larry paid no attention.

Suddenly there was a burst of movement and Larry found himself sitting dazedly against the wall. In a flash, Rebecca was kneeling beside him looking up at Arnold.

"What happened?" she asked.

Arnold replaced his glasses.

"Sorry. I did try to warn him."

He turned to face Rebecca.

"I saw you running off and thought I'd better come round straight away and explain. The girl you saw me with comes to my evening class on Wednesdays. I drop her off on the way home. Her husband is the landlord of the King's Arms and as he's old friend of mine, I usually stay and have a chat. I didn't say anything before because I thought Larry might not approve of someone who teaches karate..."

Rebecca's kiss cut him short.

Larry sheepishly picked himself up. He shook his head and grinned.

"Well! That seems to be that."
He gave Arnold a hearty slap on the back.
"Anyone for coffee?" ♦

Operation Checkout

Agatha Pringle stood at the security office window and pointed.

"That's the man," she said, quietly.

"You realise this is a very serious charge your making?"

The manager's voice was grave.

"Are you absolutely sure that it was a gun?"

Miss Pringle peered disdainfully at him over the top of her gold-rimmed spectacles.

"Certainly, young man. One sees plenty of them on the television."

The manager nodded to the security officer who handed him a truncheon from a drawer.

"Would you mind waiting here for a few moments, madam?"

"Not at all, young man." Miss Pringle placed her heavy shopping bag on a chair and sat beside it, looking anxious.

The two men left the office and, a few moments later, appeared in the supermarket below.

For several minutes they followed the man in the black homburg until, glancing furtively around, he walked purposefully towards the checkout.

Closing in from either side, they stepped close and exchanged words with him. Obediently, he led the way back between the shelves and up the stairs to the office where Miss Pringle still sat waiting nervously. As they entered, she rose slightly as though she wanted to leave.

The manager, stepped quickly forward.

"No need to worry, Mrs... er...?"

"Pringle. Miss Agatha Pringle," she volunteered, timidly.

"Ah, yes! Miss Pringle," he continued. "I'm sure that this gentleman can explain everything to our mutual satisfaction."

The security officer stepped in.

"We hope—indeed, we are certain—that there's been a mistake, sir. But, you see, this good lady is under the impression that you are... carrying a gun..."

"Oh, is that all?" Laughing, the man slid his right hand inside his overcoat. "You must mean this..."

Suddenly, the manager was staring down the barrel of a gun.

"Come on now, gents." The college accent had vanished, and he motioned with the gun. "Over against the wall and get them hands up. And as for you, lady. If you hadn't poked your nose in..."

He moved towards Miss Pringle, who gave a little squeal, and buried her face in her gloved hands, her shoulders shaking in obvious terror.

The manager stepped forward and the gun immediately swung back towards him.

"Watch it! Don't let's have no heroics, mate. I ain't going to hurt the old lady. At least, I ain't if you do as you're told." The gunmen's tone was brutal. "Right! Now how about opening that safe over there before someone gets hurt."

The manager dropped to his knees and began to fumble with the combination. Then, just as the door of the safe clicked open, the room shook to an unexpected peal of laughter.

"You should see the look on your faces."

He tossed the gun onto the desk, his accent returning to normal.

"I'm sorry, but I just couldn't resist it."

The security man snatched up the gun. His jaw dropped. The gun was as light as a feather.

Tears of laughter were running down the gunmen's face. "Totally realistic, isn't it. Just like the real thing. It's our latest novelty line. A perfect replica in metallised plastic."

"Well, I, for one, don't think it's at all funny," The manager scrambled to his feet, fuming.

The security man, only too well aware that this untimely practical joke had probably cost him his job, said nothing.

Miss Pringle looked up, obviously relieved.

"You mean we are not all going to be shot?" she asked meekly.

The 'gunman' gave a courteous half bow.

"Arthur Swinburn, Miss. My company sells novelties. See? It's a toy."

He took the gun from the security man and showed it to Miss Pringle. He returned it to the holster inside his coat just as there was a screech of brakes from outside and four policemen burst in and made their way up to the office.

"Damn!"

The manager reddened again, realising that he had set off the automatic alarm in the police station when he opened the safe. Now he would have to explain how he had been fooled.

But the sergeant was very understanding.

"Not to worry, Sir," he said. "These things do happen."

He looked at Miss Pringle and smiled.

"Well, at least we can give you a lift home."

"Oh dear! That's very kind, sergeant," said Miss Pringle, "but if you don't mind, I'd really rather not arrive home in a police car."

"Right, that's settled then," said Swinburn. "My car's in Longton Road. I'd be delighted..."

"Well, with that heavy shopping bag, we can at least offer you a lift to there. It's on the way back to the station, anyway."

Minutes later, the car pulled up on the corner of Longton Road.

Thanking the sergeant, Swinburn got out

and turned to help Miss Pringle with her shopping.

As she started to emerge, her bonnet caught the top of the door. The bonnet, and the grey wig to which it was attached, tilted sideways, revealing a dark short-back-and-sides.

Swinburn raced off up the street, closely followed by what looked like a not-very-successful Charley's Aunt.

They were soon brought down by flying tackles. The bag burst open sending hundreds of banknotes fluttering across the street.

"It was a matter of timing," the sergeant explained later.

"Charlie Gates—that's Miss Pringle to you—is a very sweet opener of safes. You left him alone long enough to open the safe—which, of course, rang the alarm at the station. When you opened it at gunpoint, it went off again. But, when the whole thing collapsed into a big joke, it never occurred to anybody that the safe had been opened twice."

He chuckled.

"Makes a dear old lady, does Charlie."

The manager pulled a face.

"Doesn't he just. I thought she was such a nice old dear, I gave her a fistful of money-off vouchers as she left." ♦

Elin

She's out there somewhere.

I know.

I can feel it.

She has to be.

I've searched for her too long and too hard to give up now.

Funny! I wouldn't have thought she'd have come back. Not after what happened.

But you can't tell about these things.

Never crowds.

She always hated crowds. A real loner. I saw that 'two's-a-crowd' look when I first came across her out in the desert.

"You lost?" I said, thinking I might tidy up the passenger seat in the truck if she'd a mind to come back to town.

"I'm fine," she said.

I should have taken her word for it.

"Twenty bucks."

The guy at the motel desk slapped a key on the counter and ignored my crack about not wanting to buy the joint.

I parked the truck in front of the chalet and opened up. The room was packed near to busting with an overworked double bed, a few dilapidated sticks of furniture that could have sold a million stories to 'True Confessions', and a cracked washbasin.

"Sure ain't no palace." I tried not to sound apologetic. After all, it was the best I could do.

"It's fine."

She'd used the word a lot in the truck on the way in.

I guess I'd done most of the talking, at that, but she seemed to agree with most everything I said. She sure was a great listener. She seemed to want to hear so much that I guess I must have told her my whole life story.

At least she knew I weren't no danger to her, not since that horse-kick when I was twelve. Nigh ten years on, and I still had a twisted spine. 'Taint that I couldn't share a dirty joke with the boys now and then, but there weren't nothing that could bring back the feelings that were awakening in me before the accident.

Hell. Women was damn nice people. I guess most of them just expected something more than I can handle.

"You want to stay?" The question took me by surprise.

"I... I guess not." It was a new experience. I couldn't think what else to say. "Thanks, anyways."

She laid one pale hand on my arm and our eyes met.

"It'll be all right."

The words seemed to come from somewhere

inside my own mind, but I knew they were hers.

A warm, comforting glow began to spread through the whole of my body. Her soft green eyes seemed to grow until they filled my entire consciousness. I felt the pain in my back and legs ease, and stirrings that had long since abandoned me began to return. It was what I'd wanted for as long as I could remember. But I was scared.

Not scared like a kid listening to Mother Nature telling him he's a man. This was the kind of scared you get in a nightmare that won't let go.

"What's happening?" The fear in my mind demanded to know. "What are you doing to me? Who are you?"

"I am Elin."

The formation of her softly unspoken thought inside my head only intensified my fear.

"What are you?"

"I am your desire. You called to me and I came."

"No. No. No." The terror bubbled up to boiling. "A stranger. A woman that I found in the desert. A woman. Nothing more."

"No. Not just a woman. I was born of your desolation, your wish for oblivion. Out there, where man-made suns have cast their shadow, that catalyst gave me this form. I am Elin. A psychomorph. I am whatever you would have me be. I wish you no harm."

I struggled for breath in an ecstasy of terror.

"If … if you mean what you say, then let me go."

She took her hand from my arm and I became aware of the claustrophobic room again, and of running… running.

I was several miles down the road with the truck engine roaring in my ears before the pains hit me again.

Pulling over to the side of the road, I switched off the engine and sat shivering, listening to the sounds of the desert night.

Gradually, the fear subsided. It slid like a shawl from my mind and I began to see things in perspective. Out there in the desert, in the heat and the dust, I hadn't been surprised to see her. I guess I was half expecting her to be there. And there she was, just as nice as you please. Not just an hallucination but flesh and blood, and God knows what all else.

I reached in the glove compartment. The old forty-five was still there, cold and heavy. My wish for oblivion. But that was before… before… Elin.

It was only then that I realised that I didn't

even remember what she looked like. It wasn't like I'd forgotten. I'd had her sitting in the truck right beside me nigh on three hours and I hadn't even noticed what she looked like.

By now, I wasn't scared any more. I just wanted to find her again and tell her that it was all right and that I understood. And I did. Understand, I mean. Like there was something had stayed behind in my head and could explain it all away. There was nothing to be scared about. Not any more.

I turned the truck around and was about halfway back to the motel when it ran out of gas. My back was hurting real bad, but I figured I could still make it on foot if I took it slow and easy. The road was pretty rough in places and the three-quarter moon hung so low that every bump cast a long shadow.

The motel's neons didn't seem to get any nearer for a long time. Just as I was getting close enough for their light to make the rocks cast a double shadow, the night was split apart by the darnedest scream I ever heard.

By the time I reached the chalet it was too late. A stringy, middle-aged woman was standing in the doorway, hands up to her face, her mouth opening and closing speechlessly. She seemed not to be breathing, choked by the terror that gripped her throat.

I pushed past her into the room and knew

at once that the scream had not been hers. Lying huddled against the end of the bed was what had once been the guy at the desk. The disarray of his clothes made it obvious what he'd had in mind just a few minutes earlier. Now he looked as though all Hell had chewed him up and spat him back out.

The woman at the door managed a long, wailing intake of breath and fell silent again, pointing hysterically into the room as if it explained everything. Then collapsing to her knees, she beat the floor with her fists.d

"It was her. She did it. He didn't mean her no harm. I told him he oughta know better than messing with them young girls at his age. Soon as he heard that truck drive off, he up an' sneaked out of the house. I followed him, just like the other times."

She paused and crawled across to cradle the fast-putrefying remains in her lap.

"He never did pay no mind to me. But I loved him. He was all I got. Used to watch them young girls through the window is all. He didn't mean no harm."

Her tears ran down the suppurating forehead and formed a pool in an empty eye-socket.

I resisted the growing temptation to throw up.

My experience with Elin had been so

different. The power that had so nearly overwhelmed me had reflected my own mood. Compassion.

I had only shown her a little kindness, yet she had offered me reward beyond my dreams. It had only been my own fear and suspicion that had broken her hold.

"Did he touch her?"

I could understand how Elin would protect herself.

The woman looked up with all the loneliness and fear of a lost child.

"He opened the door and went in. When I reached the window, he had his hands on her throat and her dress was ripped open. She didn't struggle or call out. I thought she was too scared. Then he let go of her and backed away. She reached out and held him just for a moment and her eyes... they seemed to glow... red as blood. Then he screamed, and I ran round to the door and he was just... lying there."

"What happened to Elin? The woman? Where did she go?"

There was no reply. I left her alone with her grief and searched the compound for gas for the truck. It was just about dawn when I restarted the engine and set out to find Elin.

Endless years of following a trail of other people's nightmares, searching for my dream.

Always in lonely places, never where there are crowds. It's impossible for a psychomorph to digest so many conflicting emotions.

This time, it will be all right and the pains will be gone forever.

Only Elin can make them go away.

She's out there somewhere.

I know.

I can feel it.

She has to be! ◆

<u>Phoney</u>

Phil Bates picked up his mail from the doormat. It was wet, and the ink on one of the envelopes was almost unreadable. Absentmindedly blotting it on his shirtfront, he tugged at the newspaper that was jammed through the letterbox. That, too, was wet. At least, the part of it that fell with a soggy thud onto the step outside was.

He stared in fury at the stump, making a mental note to cancel the damned thing if the delivery boy couldn't push it right in future. Opening the front door, he scooped up the pile of *papier maché* and squeezed the water out. If they didn't toe the line, somebody would get the next lot rammed right up his left nostril.

Bates picked up the milk. There were two small holes in the gold top. Those blasted birds had been at it again. Now he was in danger of contracting claw and beak disease from his bowl of cornflakes, a danger that diminished with the discovery that the cornflake packet was empty.

Settling for coffee and cremated toast, he opened the mail. Two identical brochures from a book club, a 'pay-up-or-else' from a credit-card company and a letter from his recently estranged wife, Ethel. She was coming round this afternoon to pick up her personal effects, so would he be sure not to be around so that there wouldn't be another scene.

Bates' *joie de vivre* hit a new low. At least, when Ethel had been around, there had been someone to have a go at.

He looked at the kitchen clock.

Quarter to ten.

He switched on the radio.

"That is the end of the news headlines. Now it's two minutes past twelve and time for this week's edition of our phone-in programme 'Make Your Point'".

There was the sound of a telephone ringing-tone, followed by the overbearingly cheerful voice of the presenter welcoming listeners and reciting a familiar telephone number.

"Remember, folks, that's the number to ring if you have any—and I do mean *any*—interesting observations to make on the current scene. And today, being our one-hundredth edition, is a very special day for us and for some lucky listener out there. Today, we're giving away—yes, folks—giving away one thousand pounds. Our computer will select a telephone number, completely at random and, later in the programme, we'll dial that number and give to that lucky listener one thousand pounds. If there's no reply, however, the money will go to a well-known charitable organisation..."

Bates snorted. Damned phoneys. How would the public know what happened to the money? They never name the charities. It was just a shabby ruse to get the suckers to listen to the stupid programme and that was a point that someone ought to make.

Bates picked up the phone and dialled the number. It was engaged.

An eternity passed before he got through, his ire boiling over.

"And we have another caller on Line One," came the voice of the presenter. "Hello..."

The rest was drowned by a howl from the loudspeaker.

Bates hastily turned down the volume. The howling stopped.

"Sounds like we have a newby in the seat, folks," said the voice at the other end of the phone. "Who forgot to turn down the radio, then? Naugh-ty, naughty..."

"Don't be so damned stupid," Bates barked into the phone. "I'm not one of your doting morons. If you're not able to hold an intelligent conversation, you should step down and make way for someone who is."

There was no hesitation in the other's response.

"Okay, okay. Is that your point or do you have something even more vitriolic in store for us? If so, please go right ahead. M-m-m-make

Your Point."

Bates was committed.

"You're all phoneys," he blurted. "You and all the programmes like yours. That's my point. How can you possibly justify your existence?"

The levity in the presenter's voice strengthened.

"It had to come one day, folks. No, thanks. I won't wear a blindfold. Just make it quick and clean..."

"That's exactly what I mean," snapped Bates. "How can you expect to be taken seriously if you turn everything into a joke?"

"Whoa, boy," came the quick-fire reply. "Let's just look at the problem closely and see what we've got. A little humour? Fine! Most people prefer it to a sombre note. And it has the added advantage that it gives us time to think. What a dull, dull programme we'd have if it were full of pauses for thought. Where's the entertainment in that?"

Bates had a distinct feeling that he was being put down.

"And what about the cash you give away? I've never met anyone who's ever won anything. And the charities. Why don't you name them?"

"A good point, friend, and I'm glad you asked. If we did advertise a particular organisation over the air, it wouldn't be fair to the others. Does that answer your question?"

"But you play records and then say what label it's on. That's advertising..."

"Sorry, friend, but we've just run out of time. Perhaps we can take a rain check on that one..."

The line went dead.

Bates knew he'd won. He'd hit a very sore spot.

He turned up the radio.

"So that's it, folks."

The presenter was winding up the proceedings.

"It only remains to say that our special birthday cheque for one thousand pounds *will* be going to a well-known charity after all. And the unlucky donor, whose number was engaged when we called, was a Mr Philip Bates, of Worswell. Our commiserations, Mr Bates, if you're listening. But I'm sure the money will be put to very good use..."

Bates hurled the radio into the fireplace.

"Damned phoneys," he sobbed. ◆

Parting Gift

Tracy held out the letter for the receptionist to see.

"It doesn't say why, only that I should call in at my earliest convenience," she explained.

The receptionist scanned the page briefly.

"Well, I'll see if Mr Penfold can see you, Miss Blake. He doesn't normally see anyone without an appointment. If you'd like to take a seat. He has a client with him and another due in about fifteen minutes."

Tracy was still wondering what it was all about and what Mr Penfold could possibly have to say to her that could not have been done by letter. It all seemed so casual and, judging by the receptionist's manner, more than a little unusual.

"Mr Penfold will see you now, Miss Blake."

The receptionist shepherded Tracy up thickly carpeted stairs to an even more thickly carpeted office. An elderly man in gold-rimmed glasses rose to greet her.

"I'm sure this must be as puzzling to you as it is to me," he said, ushering her to an armchair and returning to his place behind a large oak desk.

He rummaged around in a drawer and produced a flat package which he placed between them on the desk. From another drawer, he took a letter written in a bold, firm hand on startling pink paper.

"I have been instructed to ask you one or two questions, Miss Blake, the outcome of which may or may not be beneficial to you. To what extent this may be so, I am unable to say at this point. I feel sure that you will shortly be aware of the reasons for the air of mystery—yes, I think you might call it that—that currently surrounds this... er... this... er... He waved a hand over the package. "*This* is what has made it necessary for me to approach you in such an unusual manner."

Tracy felt her stomach tighten as the solicitor delivered his preamble. He seemed to sense her tension and hastily cut the string on the flat package.

"Does this mean anything to you, Miss Blake?" He slid the package across the desk. "Please think carefully. It really is most important."

Tracy lifted the lid of the box and parted layers of age-stained tissue.

"Oh!" Tears welled in her eyes. Her heart thumped as long-suppressed memories flooded back, making her oblivious to her surroundings. "Miss Toynbee. Dear Miss Toynbee. I'm so sorry. I didn't mean to hurt you. Truly, I didn't. I hoped you'd understand and forgive me so that we could be friends again. It's been so long…"

"Little girl." The voice was stern. "What exactly do you think you are doing in my garden?"

Tracy stopped searching among the shrubbery and looked to see who had spoken.

"I'm sorry," she called to the invisible complainant. "I didn't know anyone lived here."

"And did you bother to ask? Did you knock at the door, just in case? No, you most certainly did not. Neither have you answered my question, child. I asked what you were doing."

"Please, ma'am," Tracy concluded that the voice had come from a partly open window on the first floor. "I was looking for my ball. It bounced over the wall."

"It's over by the gate, right against the wall."

The window slid shut with a thud.

Tracy found the ball and picked it up. She looked up at the window and smiled towards the eyes that she knew were still watching her every movement. The curtain twitched. She smiled again and bounced the ball then, patting it along the garden path, she skipped up the steps to the front door and rang the bell.

Inside, the metallic tone echoed around empty-sounding rooms but there was no reply.

Tracy tugged again at the great iron bell-pull.

The echoes faded, again without a response. She picked up the ball and turned to leave.

She had barely reached the bottom step when bolts were slid back, and the heavy oak door creaked a few inches ajar.

"What is it now, child?" The old lady sounded irritated. "You've found your ball. Just run along and play—and try not to let it bounce into my garden again." The door closed with a bang.

"I only wanted to thank you properly," said Tracy, disappointed.

The door reopened slightly.

"And why should you want to do that?"

The voice sounded softer, a little surprised.

Tracy ran back up the steps.

"Because mummy told me that it's rude not to."

"But I haven't done anything to warrant it."

"Oh, but you have." Tracy brightened again. "You told me where my ball was—even though I hadn't asked if I could look for it. I know you didn't want me in your garden, but you weren't nasty to me like some people would have been. I wanted to meet you and thank you properly. I hoped we might be friends..."

"That was extremely presumptuous of you. What on earth made you think that I would want to be your friend?"

"Because you sounded so lonely." Tracy hesitated for a moment. "What's pre-sum-tu-ous?"

"It means, little girl, that you presume too much," the voice snapped. "Lonely, indeed!"

The door closed again.

"Oh, please," Tracy pushed open the tarnished brass letterbox and peered in. "I didn't mean to be rude. But you are, aren't you? Lonely, I mean. And I really would like to be your friend."

There was a rustle from inside the door and pale blue eyes stared piercingly out.

"What's your name, little girl?"

"Tracy. What's yours?"

"Don't be impertinent."

"I told you *my* name. Won't you tell me yours? Please?"

There was a moment's hesitation.

"Oh, very well. My name is Alice Toynbee. You may call me..." There was another short pause. "Yes, you may call me *Miss* Toynbee."

The eyes disappeared, and the door began to open slowly.

"Perhaps you're right, little... er... Tracy. Perhaps we *should* get to know one another better. How would you like to join me for a cup of tea and... if I can find some... chocolate biscuits?"

The door was opened wide and Tracy followed Miss Toynbee into the gloom of the old house.

"Why do you keep the curtains closed?" she asked in a loud whisper, finding the house creepy now that she was cut off from the sunshine.

The old lady ignored the question.

"There's no need to whisper. There's nothing to be afraid of."

Miss Toynbee led Tracy into a large drawing room.

"Tea won't be a moment. Do sit down. I won't be long."

While Miss Toynbee busied herself somewhere down the hall, Tracy wandered about the room looking at the many ornaments adorning the table and side cabinets. The paintings of animals and landscapes that filled the heavy gold-painted frames on the walls seemed, to Tracy's inexperienced eyes, to be lacking in something that she found hard to define. She turned her attention to the ornaments again. Somehow, she felt that the same was also true of them.

She was still puzzling when Miss Toynbee returned with a tray which she placed on a low table near the empty fireplace. Her apparent anger now vanished, the two were soon chatting like old friends and the mystery of the pictures gradually faded.

Tracy's thoughts were interrupted by Mr Penfold asking the receptionist to apologise to his waiting client and replaced the phone.

"I'm sorry," she said, dabbing away her tears. "It's been a long time. But I've never really forgotten. I grew very fond of Miss Toynbee. I visited her often. I asked her to tell me all about herself on several occasions but she had managed to change the subject every time. With hindsight, I believe she wanted me to discover for myself."

The solicitor raised his eyebrows and peered at her over his glasses.

"What makes you think that?"

"I'm not really sure. She allowed me to go where I pleased and seemed to trust me implicitly. Over the years, I grew to know the house very well. Then, one afternoon while she was taking a nap, I opened a cupboard which was full of clothes that looked as though they hadn't been disturbed for years. I was about to close the door when I noticed something at the back. It was a picture frame like those I had seen on that first day. I dragged it out and, as I lifted off the cloth that was draped over it, I realised what had bothered me about the other pictures. There were no portraits. No photographs. Not anywhere. This was a portrait of a young and very beautiful woman whose fine-cut features were not unlike those of Miss Toynbee. I was about to replace it when I heard a footstep behind me and Miss Toynbee caught her breath. I felt a certain coolness about her as she told me to put it back and come downstairs.

"When I arrived in the lounge, she told me to sit down and not to interrupt. She went on to tell me how she had once met a young RAF pilot on the base where she was stationed as a WAAF during the war. He had the portrait painted to mark their engagement. Then, just a few days before they were to be married, there was an air attack on the base and the operations room ceiling collapsed. She was very badly burned and had to undergo a series of painful facial operations. She never saw her fiancé again, and everyone carefully changed the subject whenever she asked about him. She was sure that he had been killed but, although she didn't find out the whole story until after the war, he had been posted to another station at his own request. He couldn't bear the thought of having to see the terrible scarring on her face day after day."

Mr Penfold listened intently as Tracy went on.

"Perhaps I was too young to understand. I found it difficult to believe that she could still love him after he'd deserted her. But, somehow, she felt that the portrait was the way he would always remember her and that was why she had kept it for all these years. But she shared his fears about the dreadful scars left by the operations. She had thrown out every mirror in the house and shut herself away from people.

I tried to tell her that there were no visible scars any more, that she was still beautiful and that he didn't deserve her. But she refused to listen.

"I didn't see her for a few days, then my father was transferred to another office and we had to move away. I was very sad at the thought of leaving Miss Toynbee alone again. She had become very special to me and I thought very hard about what she'd told me. I bought this mirror as a parting gift. I hoped that, when she saw her reflection she'd see that there were no scars any more."

Tracy's eyes filled with tears again and her voice trembled.

"When she opened the box, she seemed paralysed for a moment. She went very white and glared as though she hated me. She called me a spiteful little girl. Her voice was very low and quite firm. I was so surprised and so dreadfully hurt that I burst into tears and ran from the room with her calling after me that she never wanted to see me again. I did write to her after we had moved but she didn't reply."

While Tracy composed herself, Mr Penfold took out another letter.

"Miss Toynbee did reply, in actual fact," he said. "But she didn't post it. What you've told me this morning is just what I hoped you would say. I had to be sure that you are, indeed, the Tracy Blake that we have been trying to locate for some time now. This is the letter you would have received if you had not been so distracted that you forgot to include your new address."

Tracy's eyes widened in surprise as the solicitor handed her the envelope. The letter was dated 1998.

"My Dear Tracy," it read. "I am so sorry for the way I treated you during your last visit. I know, beyond any shadow of doubt, that you gave me the mirror as a token of affection and not, as I saw it at the time, as an instrument of spite. If I had retained even a fraction of your young innocence, I would have realised that such an act was not in you and that you were totally incapable of lying to me. I hope that you will forgive a stupid, obstinate old woman and that we can once again enjoy the friendship that has given us both so much pleasure." It was signed, "With very sincere regret, Alice Toynbee."

"Miss Blake, I'm sorry to tell you that Miss Toynbee... er... passed away almost two years ago. She was insistent, right to the end, that we should try to locate you and to deliver that letter. Her will, which I also have here, names you as the sole heir to her not inconsiderable estate..."

Mr Penfold waited for the news to sink in.

Tracy carefully folded the letter and put it into her handbag.

"I did lie to her, you know. She really wasn't beautiful, even all those years after the operations. There were still scars. But I did so want her to believe that she was still beautiful that I came to believe it myself. I'd really rather remember her the way she was when I knew her, Mr Penfold. Do you think she'd mind if I have the portrait destroyed?" ♦

Rear View

A different man any time she wanted one.

She had said it almost as soon as Stephen had opened his eyes after the accident. He couldn't reply, couldn't call for help even after all the tubes had been removed. There was too much pain. Too much sedation to understand clearly what Maria vowed in the seclusion of the tiny private ward.

But, over the months, the words had crystallized in Stephen's mind. At first, like the pain, his mind had shut them out but, somehow, they had broken through, turning his once-tender love to hatred.

Futility burned as he moved the tiny joystick that controlled the wheelchair. The motor whirred as the chair rolled out of the room and along the passage to his bedroom. As the door swung open, the dazzling rays of the setting sun from across the valley blinded him momentarily, reminding him of the night of the accident.

Good business, good food and good wine had spurred Stephen homewards. His beloved Maria would be waiting, and their celebration would be ecstatic.

The whole valley was bathed in the orange rays that spelt the end of day, and his heart leapt at the sight of his house on the hillside opposite, where he and Maria would soon be sharing each other's delights.

He moved his head slightly to avoid the rays of the setting sun in the rear-view mirror. Then, as he rounded the final bend, a flash of fire blinded him, and the wheel slipped in his hands. He gripped it tight. Too tight.

The front wheels started to slide. His foot found the brake and the car spun, hit a rock and rolled towards the edge as blackness engulfed him.

For four long years, there had been no escape from Maria's constant recriminations; accusations of betrayal; of incompetence; of depriving her of all that his success had promised. She vowed that his mountain retreat would become a prison where he would live out her retribution.

Now, while she was away seeking her pleasures in the city, Stephen took stock of his abilities. Totally paralysed except for the smallest of movements in his right hand, he was completely dependent on the chair for his mobility and upon Maria, who had dismissed the private nurse, for his bodily needs. Even if he could have spoken, the telephone had been removed 'so that he would not be disturbed', and the removal of radio and television had completed his isolation.

In defence of his sanity, Stephen's still-brilliant mind focused every waking thought on finding relief from this most evil of existences.

Slowly regaining control, Stephen realised that his tears were not of emotion but the result of the flash of sunlight. He tried to blink away the purple haze that wandered slowly across his field of vision, and, as he wondered why the sun had apparently changed its angle, the reason slowly became apparent.

Across the room, the half-open wardrobe door was redirecting the sun's rays towards him.

Careful not to look into the mirror, he steered around the bed and pushed the wardrobe door shut with the footrest.

As he pulled away, the footrest caught under the edge of the door, causing the motor to complain and the tyres to screech on the parquet floor. The movement lifted the front of the wardrobe slightly. As the chair broke free, the wardrobe swivelled on one corner, painting the room with blinding light. It rocked for a moment then toppled, crushing him sideways against the bed.

Stephen became aware of movement around him. Bright lights and quiet, efficient voices. And the touch of crisp, clean sheets.

He felt gentle pressure of fingers on his wrist and opened his eyes. The tall, blonde nurse looked up from her fob-watch and smiled.

"You've had a very lucky escape," she said. "I know you can't talk, Mr Parkin. Just blink if you understand."

Stephen blinked—and squeezed her hand.

The nurse stared for a moment then called the doctor.

"It was like a kind of warmth as the wardrobe fell on me. Then I passed out," Stephen explained later as the nurse puffed up his pillows.

"The policeman who found you is waiting outside," said the nurse. "Do you feel strong enough to see him?"

The policeman drew up a chair.

"I'm sure your wife wouldn't have suffered, sir," he said. "The driver of the car behind said there was a brilliant flash of light from a house across the valley, possibly from the mirror as the wardrobe fell on you. She must have been dazzled by it. She went over the edge at the same bend where your accident happened."

Stephen shifted his position and tried not to smile. ♦

Maggie Pander

Hugh Weeny pulled himself up to his full, portly five-feet-four and swayed ever so slightly.

"Nonsense, officer. I am by no means under the influence of alcohol."

"Yes, sir," said the desk Sergeant, stroking his bald pate with the butt of one flustered hand.

"Caught 'im talking to a lamppost outside the park, Serge," said Constable Higgins, taking out his notebook and letting go of Weeny's arm. "At approximately eleven-fifty-seven this evening, I was proceeding along Park Road in a..."

"Cut it short, Higgins," interjected the weary Sergeant.

"...Westerly direction, in pursuit of my duty..."

"Short, Higgins!"

"Well, Serge, I saw him talking to this lamp post, so I nicked him. Drunk and disorderly."

"Rubbish!" said Weeny. "Codswallop, piffle and... balderdash! I was talking to a friend."

The Sergeant leaned across the desk as though he was about to learn the secret of the universe.

"And the name of this friend, sir?"

"Maggie Pander, Sergeant." Weeny's soft

brown eyes gazed, spaniel-like, into the Sergeant's spectacles. "We're from Mars..."

"Hmm! Mars, eh? Which part?"

"Cretalus. Near Molik."

A smile spread across the sergeant's thin face.

"Lovely spot this time of year, sir."

Weeny looked nostalgic.

"Yes... until the developers moved in. Have you been there recently?"

"Not for a couple of hundred years, sir. Thought about it, though. Often. Maybe one day... Who can tell?"

Constable Higgins stared in disbelief, first at one then the other.

"Serge. I don't want to interrupt..."

"Then don't!"

"But...?"

"Tell you what, Higgins. Perhaps a nice cup of tea for Mr Weeny while we sort this out."

"Mmm? That's very kind of you, Sergeant."

"Not at all, sir. But I must ask you to empty your pockets first. You know... The rules?"

Relieved, Higgins realised that Weeny was being strung along.

A small collection of articles gathered on the desk: wallet, handkerchief, small change... and a large green crystal.

"Lucky charm?" he asked.

Weeny held up the crystal.

"All Martians carry one of these. It's our only means of getting back home. I suppose you'd call it 'teleportation'."

"That's not what I'd call it," thought Higgins. "Nutty as a fruitcake, this one."

"You wouldn't believe what you can do with one of these, constable."

Higgins resisted making a suggestion.

"We travel all over the universe, just by thinking about where we want to be. Look, I'll show you..."

The sergeant's hand closed around the object.

"Perhaps later, sir, if you don't mind."

He nodded towards the interview room and Higgins escorted Weeny along the corridor. In a few moments he was back.

"Right! Shall I check the local nuthouse to see if he's escaped."

The Sergeant was putting Weeny's belongings into a large brown envelope.

"So... you think he's a nut?"

"Yes. Daft as a brush..."

The sergeant sealed the envelope and attached the list to it.

"And what's so daft about a brush?"

He grinned at the other's expression.

"Look at it this way, lad. A bloke says he comes from Mars. You think he's potty. But you booked him for being drunk. I didn't smell any drink on his breath..."

"But...?"

"No, just a minute. If you're going to make a good copper, you mustn't jump to conclusions. He might be telling the truth. Unlikely, yes! Or it might be what he believes to be the truth. And that doesn't make him legally insane... Yes, madam?"

Higgins jumped as the sergeant turned to face a short, plump, jolly-looking woman. She smiled.

"I wonder if you can help me. I'm looking for a... a Mr Weeny."

It was Higgins' turn to smile.

"Oh, the man from Mars," he blurted.

"That's enough, Higgins," snapped the Sergeant. "Sorry, madam, you were saying?"

"That's perfectly all right, Sergeant. He does spin a bit of a yarn, but he's quite harmless, I assure you. May I see him?"

"Certainly, madam. Your name, please?"

"Maggie Pander, Sergeant. He is all right, is he?"

"Yes, madam. Take the lady along, Higgins."

As the two figures disappeared along the corridor, the sergeant opened the envelope, removed the contents and fed them, one by one, into the fire which burned brightly in one corner of the office.

Suddenly, the crash of breaking crockery echoed along the corridor and Higgins returned, breathless.

"Hey, Serge, they've gone. Vanished!"

The Sergeant smiled.

"Thought they might," he said. "Couldn't very well search her to see if she was carrying one of these. Not without a policewoman to carry out the search, eh?"

The green crystal sparkled as he held it up.

He noticed the near-tearful look on the other's face. "Never mind, son. Best forget it ever happened."

The crystal touched the Sergeant's temple. Higgins felt a momentary giddiness and found that he was standing with the sergeant outside the park. He rubbed his eyes. When he opened them, nothing had changed. The road was deserted except for themselves.

The sergeant's voice took on a fatherly air.

"Sorry, son. These things can take you back in time, too. It's just coming up to eleven-fifty-five; just before you first saw Mr Weeny. Only, this time, you won't." He raised the crystal again. "I lost mine back in 1746. I really couldn't miss this opportunity to get back home."

"Home?"

"Mars! You won't remember a thing."

The uniformed figure flickered for a

moment then vanished.

Constable Higgins pulled up his coat collar. It was chilly at this hour. He shivered and blew on his fingers.

He thought he saw a movement in the shadows under a lamp. He went over. There was no one there.

He put on his gloves and looked along the empty street.

"Nothing interesting ever happens on this beat." ◆

No Hope in Hell

I killed Danver. I didn't mean to, it just happened.

I'd reached the end of the line and he just had to interfere.

If he hadn't poked his nose in, it would all have been over now.

How did I ever get into this mess?

It's only two days since I made up my mind to break out of this hick town for good; to get away from this hell where every day is no different from any other and time has no beginning and no end.

If I didn't make it this time, perhaps when they found my body they'd understand. But, by then, I'd be past caring.

Then it happened again, just like all those other times.

When I arrived at the bus station when they told me there'd be more buses to anywhere for a while. Something about the road being out.

I hung around for a couple of hours but, whenever they saw me coming, they just shook their heads apologetically. In the end I couldn't stand it any longer. That's when Danver interfered. He didn't even leave me any choice when it came to killing myself. He must have been spying on me, the way he burst in like that. Anyway, without stopping to argue with him, I kicked out. Hard. It took him completely off guard. His head snapped back and down he went, slamming into the wall as he fell.

No need to look twice. At that angle, his neck had to be broken.

I ran.

Suddenly the only thing that mattered was to save my own skin.

I suppose it was funny in a way. You know, funny that someone on the verge of suicide should panic when they find themselves in danger.

At the outskirts of the town I sat on a rock, feeling the panic begin to ebb. The desert sand simmered just below the boil and I found myself wondering how long a man could last out there. Somehow, I knew that no-one had ever crossed it on foot. I was trapped in a natural prison.

Then another thing occurred to me. I was sharing my prison with Danver's body. If I didn't do something about it pretty quick, I hadn't a hope in hell.

But somebody had beaten me to it. When I arrived back at the apartment, Danver's body was gone. Now, it was only a matter of time.

The panic started again. How much time? An hour? Two, perhaps?

Then it dawned on me. The rope was gone, too. And the chair, the one I'd been standing on when I kicked out at Danver, that was back in its usual place against the wall. So whoever had discovered the body also knew what I had been about to do when he burst in.

My first reaction was to doubt my own sanity. I remembered only too clearly how it happened. But had it? Could it be that my mind had gone at last, and that Danver was still out there?

Something glinted at me from behind a leg of the chair. Picking it up, I looked at it closely. A tiny gear-wheel. Probably out of Danver's watch. It must have got smashed when he fell.

So I wasn't mad after all. It really had happened. Whoever had tidied the place up had missed it.

I smiled to myself.

It was the first time in years. A satisfied smile that would have told any onlooker that I didn't give a damn about Danver, just as long as my mind wasn't coming off at the hinges.

A plan, that's what was needed. But, first things first. Sleep was most important right at the moment. It was unlikely that anyone would expect me to return to the scene of the crime so soon.

After the tension, relief flooded through me. I soon fell into a deep and dreamless sleep and, this morning, things looked a lot different.

After all, I thought, Perhaps if I could

convince them of the truth; that it had indeed been an accident.

But then again, why should I? As things were, there were two possibilities.

First, Danver was dead. In which case, for whatever reason, somebody had gone to a great deal of trouble to conceal the fact. Or, secondly, he was alive. In which case there was no reason to give myself up. Anyway, I might end up in jail for trying to commit suicide.

"So," I muttered. "He didn't serve breakfast this morning."

Danver had always been so punctual. And there was that phrase he always used. The only words I had ever heard him say.

"Will there be anything else, sir?"

So supercilious, so unfeeling. It had a metallic timbre as though it had just come out of a tin; as though he'd picked it off a shelf.

"No. He must be dead. So why haven't I been arrested?" I said aloud.

As though in reply, there was a familiar tap at the door. It opened slowly. Standing there, breakfast tray poised for me to take, was Danver. He looked just the same as always, as though nothing had happened.

My legs felt suddenly weak and I sank onto the edge of the bed, only to jump up again in surprise as Danver let go of the tray.

"Will there be anything else, sir?" he

chimed, apparently oblivious to the mess he'd just made on the floor. Then, without waiting for an answer, he moved off down the corridor leaving me to stare after his retreating form. He swayed heavily with every step and, reaching the top of the stairs, strode forward as though to carry straight on.

His flight to the bottom ended in a sickening thud but, before I could reach him, he was on his feet again.

"Are you all right?" I started to ask.

"Will there be anything else, sir?" His voice seemed more mechanical than ever.

"Will there be anything else, sir?"

He repeated the phrase again and again.

That was when I noticed that he was not opening his mouth when he spoke, and I remembered the gear-wheel.

Without it, Danver's delicate mechanism failed to work properly.

I've gone over the whole story a hundred time and now it makes a kind of sense.

Strange voices, somewhere inside my head, tell me that I'm the only human on Altair IV and all the other people are androids—like Danver.

Now that I know, I'm to have a mate, taken from a place called Earth to join me in this alien zoo. Her memories will be erased as mine were.

She must never learn what I have learned and, for her sake alone, I must survive. ♦

Special Occasion

Emily Wilson smoothed down on an imaginary wrinkling in her neat green dress and smiled at her reflection in the wardrobe mirror. It was not a conceited smile, for Emily never considered herself to be worthy of conceit. There was a kind of companionship; a sense of being in the company of another, separated only by the surface of the glass.

For the first time in all her 38 years, Emily was conscious of the need to share her life with someone else. Now, perhaps, that need might be fulfilled. If only...

Her fingers gently traced a faint line of a scar which ran from her left eyebrow and disappeared into the grey hair above her temple. Would he notice? Would he...?

Emily flushed. How silly! If he had not noticed by now, he must be blind. But don't they say that love is...?

Emily's heart skipped at the thought. Oh, God! Could it be possible?

Her memory raced back through the years.

Yes, she thought, once there had been love.

For a moment, she recalled the exhilaration of that summer day just before her twentieth birthday; the wind tugging at her dark hair as it streamed out behind her; her arms tight around Graham as he crouched over the handlebars, the hedges roaring past as he opened the throttle.

Emily drew in a sharp breath and covered her face with her hands.

With love had come pain. One moment the lane was empty, then a tractor had appeared from nowhere and blocked the road completely. Mercifully, there had never been any doubt that Graham had died instantly.

For two months they had kept the news from Emily until she had recovered sufficiently to stand the shock.

But the physical pain had only been a foretaste of the mental anguish that had followed. The true miracle was that she had retained her sanity.

Since then, Emily had built a wall around herself, turning her world into a sanctuary into which entry was strictly limited. But, over the past few months, there had been a visitor to the garden.

Emily felt a warm glow of contentment at the very thought of her new-found relationship with Peter. His daily call had become the focal point in her otherwise drab existence. Her ears would strain to catch the gentle chink of bottles which always heralded the approach of his milk float. The gate would creak open and footsteps would scrunch along the gravel path to the accompaniment of his carefree whistling.

"Morning, Miss Emily."

There was always that special something about the way he said it.

"And how's my best girl today, then?"

It had started as a light-hearted greeting but, as time passed, the insincerity vanished along with the wink that had once accompanied the words. Now, there was a sense of tradition; a bond that had brought together two lonely people.

Emily was so sure that they were right for each other. Peter's happy facade might hide his true feelings from the world at large but, to Emily's sensitive perception, he was as transparent as glass. His carefully chosen words made it obvious that he, too, felt insecure in his relationship with other people. That alone was enough to convince Emily that it was she who must make the first move. And what better opportunity would present itself than her own birthday.

She looked at the clock on the bedside table. 10:23. He would be here, as usual, promptly at 10:50, only today... well... today would be different. Coffee and biscuits would await his arrival, and perhaps a slice of the cake that Emily had baked especially for the occasion. No candles, of course. They were of no importance.

Trembling slightly with anticipation, Emily glanced once more in the mirror. Then, satisfied that she was ready, turned and left the room.

At the foot of the stairs, she stopped to pick up the local newspaper from the doormat, where it had lain since before breakfast. Placing it on a stool in the kitchen, she busied herself with the preparation of freshly percolated coffee and soon the aroma had permeated throughout the whole house.

Realising that everything was ready with several minutes to spare, Emily started leafing casually through the newspaper. And there, in the centre of one page, was a photograph of Peter.

After the first surprise, Emily's reaction was to panic. Something dreadful must have happened to him. But, to her great relief, a quick glance at the caption reminded her that she was behaving like a schoolgirl with her first crush

'Milkman voted top tradesmen' it ran. 'In our recent poll to find the most popular tradesmen in...' so that was it, called Emily. She read on. As she did so, doubts began to enter her mind. It seemed that Peter had received most of his votes from housewives who've been influenced by his natural ability to make them feel 'feminine'. So, it was not only she who had experienced the feeling.

Emily's moist eyes found the small type increasingly difficult to read. She caught a fleeting glimpse of the phrase '... lives with his family in...', and then the tears came.

Dropping the paper, Emily ran upstairs and threw herself down on the bed. So he was married, after all. Why had he never once mentioned his wife? 'Family', the paper had said. That meant children, too.

She lay for a few moments refusing to let her emotions give way, denying herself the relief of breaking down completely. After all, that will solve nothing.

This was stupid, she told herself sternly. Why on earth should he have told her all about his private life, anyway? She could feel her old more cynical self taking control again. Just a few minutes ago she had actually preened herself before the mirror in this very room. And for what? So that she might make a good impression on someone else's husband. It was almost pathetic. She sat up and wiped her eyes.

No! This time, it will not be allowed to hurt and, hearing the familiar sounds of the milk float rounding the corner brought Emily face-to-face with the immediate situation. There was nothing else for it but to carry on as though nothing had happened.

It would be impossible to avoid seeing him again, and trying to would only make things worse. And besides, he hadn't done anything wrong. If she had become too infatuated, she had only herself to blame.

That was the gate opening. If she hurried, by the time she reached the back door, Peter would be just about to knock.

"Morning, Miss Emily." His blue eyes twinkled. "You're looking particularly nice this morning. Special occasion?"

"My birthday," Emily found herself saying, surprised at her acceptance of the situation. "And it isn't every day that you get your picture in the paper. It only arrived a few minutes ago. And as we've both got something to celebrate, I thought you might like a cup of coffee. It's all ready."

"Well, thank you, Miss Emily. That's very kind of you." Peter removed his peaked cap and stepped inside. "It can be thirsty work at times."

Emily asked about the contest. Peter laughed.

"Well, to tell you the truth," he said, "I didn't know anything about it until the chap came out the other evening to take the photo. I thought he was having me on at first. I must say, It's so nice of everyone. Look at this."

He took an envelope out of his wallet.

"They presented me with two tickets for a West End show and dinner at a posh restaurant. And I was wondering..." he hesitated. "I wonder if you do me honour of accompanying me?"

"But...?" Emily could have choked on the words. "What about your wife? The paper said that you were married."

Peter laughed out loud. "Bless you, Miss Emily, but it didn't. I live with my parents. That's what they meant by family."

Emily could have wept for joy. "Then of course I'd be delighted to come," she said. Then she added: "but only on condition that you stop calling me 'Miss'..."

Peter looked a little sheepish for a moment, then he reached down and laid his hand on hers.

"For months," he said, "I've been trying to summon up the courage to ask you out. Now it really will be a special occasion." ♦

Table for Three

Sheila wiped her rubber-gloved hands and picked up the telephone receiver with a minimum of fingers.

"Two three eight four six."

"Sheila. Won't be able to make it back in time for dinner tonight."

Sheila sighed with exasperation.

"Oh, not again, darling. It's Christmas Eve and you know Jane and Robert are coming to dinner. It's been arranged for ages. I can't just put them off at a moment's notice. How late do you think you'll be?"

"Can't say. The roads are pretty awful and it's getting worse."

There was a pause. Sheila thought she heard someone whispering against the steady rhythm of windscreen wipers. The phone crackled.

"Paul? Paul, are you there?"

No reply. The even note of the engine changed for a moment and was broken by a high-pitched chuckling sound.

"Paul?

"Sorry, darling. Had to put the phone down to take a corner. Made the tyres squeal a bit.

"What time *will* you be home?"

"Can't say. Maybe not until late. Last minute call. I've got to tie up a contract before the holiday. Could be an all-night session. Apologies to Jane and your brother. Bye-ee."

The chuckling sound came again just as the line clicked dead.

Sheila stared at the receiver in frustration and slammed it down. Was it too much to expect your husband to be home on time? They'd moved out to the country to get away from the pressures of big-city life. Perhaps that had been a mistake after all.

Two hours had passed by the time Sheila's anger had turned to resignation. The clock on the sideboard showed six o'clock. With any luck, Paul would be on his way home by now. It would be a pity if he really couldn't make it in time. She picked up the phone and dialed his number.

Although having a mobile was useful, Sheila had never liked the idea. She'd always been afraid that Paul would be distracted by it. But it improved efficiency, or so the Company said. That was as may be, but it had certainly meant longer hours. There was no reply.

Sheila busied herself with the final preparations for dinner. She couldn't bring herself to lay the table for three. She had seen little enough of Paul lately as it was. Almost as though he had a permanent excuse for not being home on time.

The cold December rain had turned to sleet which lashed at the windows. Jane and Robert were due at eight o'clock. It seemed almost a pity to bring them out on a night like this if Paul wouldn't be here.

The table looked most inviting; the flowers, the unlit candles, and the glittering silverware reflecting soft, warm lighting. Sheila drew the curtains and shut out the unbidding night. Time for a sherry before popping the chicken chasseur into the oven.

The warm glow of the sherry rivaled that of the hissing log fire. Sparks traced intricate lacework across the throat of the chimney, as though to add a little Christmas cheer to the blackness of the soot—dark and forbidding like the night outside. She sank back into the embracing depths of the armchair, feeling the tensions of the past few hours melt away.

Keys rattled in the front door. Sheila sat up in alarm.

"Paul?" Who else could it be? "Paul? Is that you?"

There was no reply, but she could hear movement in the hall. A tightness in her throat ignored her natural reticence to believe that anything was wrong. She tried vainly to call out again, more to dispel her own fears than to challenge the newcomer. No sound came.

Like a child awaiting chastisement, Sheila drew her legs up into the safety of the chair and waited, her heart beating faster as a shadow fell across the partly open door into the hall. She crouched further back into the chair as the door swung open and a tall, bedraggled figure stood silhouetted against the brighter light.

"Paul!"

Sudden relief made Sheila laugh as the fear of just a few moments earlier vanished like a bubble in a flame.

"Darling, you're drenched."

The observation was superfluous. Pools were already forming on the shiny parquet as an almost constant stream of water dripped from Paul's clothes. Sheila jumped up out of the chair and placed her unfinished sherry on the mantelpiece.

"You'd better get out of those wet things before you catch your death. I'm so glad you managed to get back in time after all. I did try to ring you, but I couldn't get through. I was beginning to think you'd found yourself another woman, what with all the overtime you've been putting in lately."

The words seemed to be spilling out without thinking.

"There was an accident." Paul's voice was flat and matter-of-fact.

"Oh. dear. What sort of accident?" At least Paul was all right. "Let me get you a towel, darling, and you can tell me all about it while you change. You're making an awful mess on the floor."

Taking a towel from the airing cupboard, she sat Paul on a kitchen stool and rubbed at his hair. He was very pale and obviously dazed. His eyes were glazed, and his pupils dilated. Sheila felt his forehead, it was cold. He must have been very shaken by the accident. Best get him out of his wet clothes as soon as possible.

She led him to the bathroom, trailing water across the hall and up the stairs. Helping him undress, she dumped his wet clothes in the bath and took down her own pink toweling bathrobe from the back of the door and wrapped him in it.

"I'm sorry," he said.

Sheila smiled. There was something so endearing and child-like about the sight of Paul in the ridiculously small bathrobe.

"Nothing to be sorry about, darling, as long as you're all right." She kissed his cold forehead. "You still haven't told me what happened."

"I was just entering a bend on the approach to the estuary,"

Paul's voice seemed a little stronger now.

"The mobile rang. I reached for it and misjudged the bend. It was pouring with rain and the road was slippery. You always said you were afraid it might happen, and you were right."

He paused as though choosing his words carefully.

"You were right about something else as well..."

"Oh, what was that?"

"There *was* someone else in the car with me."

Sheila sat on the edge of the bath, her stomach tensing at the revelation.

Paul pre-empted her question.

"No. No-one you'd know. I met her through work."

Sheila's mouth opened and closed in speechless disbelief. She became acutely aware of the smallness of the room, the pungent smell of the wet clothes, and of the gulf that had suddenly and so cruelly appeared between herself and this... this stranger. This was not the Paul she loved, this man in a pink bathrobe, who studied her so dispassionately from a few feet away. But she could find no tears. There was just a dreadful emptiness as though everything that she had ever loved had suddenly been torn from her.

Several seconds passed before Sheila took a

deep breath and stood up, smoothing inconsequential wrinkles from her dress.

"I have to put the dinner in the oven", she said, and went downstairs.

Sheila was aware of Paul watching her from the hall doorway, but she felt no urge to look round. She put the casserole dish into the oven and closed the door, deliberately standing with her back to him.

"I'm so sorry," she heard him say. "You would have found out very soon anyway. I wanted you to hear it from me, not from someone else. Truly, I didn't mean to hurt you."

"What about her?" The question demanded to be asked,

"She's waiting for me in the car."

"Then you'd better not keep her waiting any longer, had you."

Sheila gripped the edge of the working surface in an effort not to turn and throw her arms around him, begging him to stay.

The door closed quietly behind her. Taking off her apron, she went through to the dining room.

The immaculately laid table now seemed, somehow, out of place. Clearing away Paul's place-setting, she put the cutlery back into the canteen on a side table and rearranged the table for three.

Then, picking up her unfinished sherry, she

curled up in the armchair and watched the fire making lace.

The logs in the fireplace settled with a rustle, interrupting Sheila's jumbled thoughts. She remembered the mess in the hall. Better clear it up before the others arrive.

Lucky it hasn't left a stain on the polish, she thought as she rinsed out the floor cloth and turned her attention to the wet clothes in the bath. Somewhere out there, Paul would be sharing this dreary night with someone else, leaving her to clean up the mess.

She was halfway down the stairs when the door-chime sounded. That would be Jane and Robert, a few minutes early despite the rain. Whatever could she say to them?

They'd have to know eventually. But perhaps tonight was not the time. Best not spoil their evening.

Sheila took a deep breath and opened the door.

"Mrs Betteridge?" A tall police sergeant and a young policewoman were standing in the rain.

"May we come in, madam? I'm afraid there's been an accident."

Sheila nodded and showed them into the hall.

"Were pretty sure that we've identified the driver from a passport we found in his briefcase... I'm afraid it looks like it was your husband, madam."

The words came in waves as nausea gripped Sheila's whole being. She struggled to find her voice as the policewoman helped her to a chair.

"Wh... what happened?"

"They must have skidded on the icy road. We had to drag the car out of the estuary. They were drowned. I'm afraid, madam. Both of them."

"They? You said 'they'."

"Yes. His passenger. We haven't yet been able to identify her yet but there was a young lady with him."

Sheila felt the room begin to spin.

"When did it happen?"

The sergeant consulted his notebook.

"As near as we can make it, Ma'am, it would be about... what? Two hours ago, I reckon. That would make it just about six o'clock."

Sheila put a shaking hand to her mouth and the tears began to come.

"There is just one other thing, Mrs Betteridge."

The policewoman produced a small pack from her tunic pocket and handed Sheila a tissue. Her voice was gentle and comforting.

"We'd might have a clearer picture of what happened if you could just tell us why your husband was wearing a pink bathrobe." ♦

Sisters

It wasn't usually so difficult to sleep as the tube train clattered and jerked its way beneath the dark streets of London. I had never really come to terms with the feeling of isolation that I experienced every Wednesday night after a long evening lecturing on ancient civilisations and beliefs at the university. True, I could have taken a taxi, but that would cost more than I earned for my evening's work.

Professor of Comparative Theology is a fine name for a post that is rich in kudos and very poor in coin. I was fully aware that alone in the last carriage of the last train across town was not the sensible place to be. Strange things can happen. Nasty things. Every day, the newspapers would report muggings, murders and worse that had happened in just such circumstances. But, somehow, I had fallen into this weekly routine and grasped the opportunity to go over the highlights of the evening in my mind. Eventually, fatigue would bob to the surface, and I would drift off into a shallow sleep. Since my destination was at the end of the line, there was always someone there to wake me if need be.

Tonight, the feeling of being so alone seemed to play on my mind. Even the stations seemed unnaturally quiet. The opening and closing of automatic doors at empty platforms added to the feeling of unease, and a sensation that I might be the only living soul grew with every stop.

As the train left Bethnal Green and picked up speed, the door to the next carriage crashed open and two youths burst in.

They stamped past, apparently unaware of my presence and, engaged in raucous and obscene conversation, sprawled across facing seats in the centre of the carriage.

Mile End came and went without incident.

The profanities paused occasionally to allow the pair time to empty cans of lager into drooling mouths, and belch loudly before continuing.

Suddenly, both heads turned in my direction and I felt my heart sink in anticipation of a page five headline in tomorrow's paper.

"Hello, then! And what we got 'ere then?"

The nearer of the two louts, probably six feet tall with bleached, scrubbing-brush hair and round shoulders, started unsteadily along the carriage. The other, broader but some two inches shorter, with a shaven head and copiously tattooed arms, reached up to the handrail and swung into the gangway to follow him.

They stood and leered at me; swaying more,

I thought, from the effects of the lager than from the movement of the train.

My only way out was through the connecting door to the next carriage. It would have been pointless trying to escape by that route but my fearful glance in that direction acted like a signal to the pair. The taller one leapt forward and, steadying himself with one hand on the back of the seat, he leaned over me and grabbed my tie and shirt-front with the other, pulling me close and belching bad breath and the overpowering smell of lager in my face.

"Where is it, then?" he growled, yanking me to my feet.

By the time I realised what he meant, the other had removed my wallet from my hip pocket.

"'Ere y'are, Smeg," he said, and waved it triumphantly.

I was pushed roughly back into the seat, with Smeg's heavy boot planted firmly and painfully in my lap to ensure that I remained there while they examined their find. I tried to avoid congratulating myself that I carried my credit cards in another pocket in case I might give something away.

Suddenly, Smeg noticed the nickel-plated clip that attached my university identity card to the inside pocket of my jacket.

He tugged at it, ripping the pocket and the jacket lining in the process. "Well, now. Ain't that a blast? Perfessor, eh? Bleedin' awful picture. What'ya fink, Caz?"

He tossed the card to his mate.

"You ought'a sue 'em for damages. That's what I fink."

Caz laughed and flicked the card at me. The clip struck the back of my hand hard enough to draw blood. I winced and both youths roared with laughter.

Disappointed at finding nothing of interest, Smeg sent the empty wallet spinning back in my direction and tossed the contents into the air letting them fall like oversized confetti around the compartment.

"Mobile?"

His abruptness made me wonder at the sudden question. His brows furrowed. He held out a hand towards me and spat out the word again. This time there was no mistaking the menace in his tone.

"I... I... I... don't have one..."

"An' you a perfessor? Can't be that bleedin' important then can yer? It's fings like that what ruins my faif in the educational system." He looked round at his companion."

"Fink we oughta do him over and see if 'e's lyin', Cas, or d'ya reckon he's tellin' the truf? I reckon we ought'a fink about it for a bit an' then we can decide what to do.”

They both laughed, as though to underline their intentions.

Without taking his eyes off me, Smeg reached above and behind him with one hand. Caz shoved a new can of lager into it. Shaking the can as he brought it round, Smeg tugged at the ring-pull, sending a blast of lager across the carriage. They both laughed as it hit me full in the face.

Too scared to do anything but blink away the sticky foam, I sat trembling, letting it dribble from the tip of my beard.

A sudden extra pressure from Smeg’s boot announced that we were approaching the next station. The boot was quickly withdrawn.

“Right,” he said, leaning across and patting my cheek firmly several times with each blow falling harder than the last in time with his words. “Just.. you... sit... quiet... an’... you’ll... be... all... right... O... K?”

I was not about to argue.

The train rumbled into Stratford station and stopped. The doors hissed open and I caught sight of an attractive woman in dark glasses who was about to board. Summoning up what little courage I could find, I made as though to shout a warning to her. Smeg’s hand went to his pocket and a knife glinted. I remained silent.

The woman moved towards the back of the carriage, taking a seat on the same side as myself, out of my direct line of sight although, as the train moved into the tunnel, I could see her clear reflection in the carriage window opposite.

As the train picked up speed, Smeg signaled to his companion, and they started along the carriage to stand directly in front of the woman.

Apparently unperturbed by their presence, the woman ignored the obvious threat, looking neither at one nor the other.

The incessant rumble and clatter of the train prevented me from hearing what was being said but there was a rapid burst of seemingly threatening words from the thugs. The woman's reflection did not move, and I saw Smeg lean down with obvious intent. The woman spoke, so softly that her voice was totally lost in the background noise. The two thugs looked at each other and laughed aloud. Smeg turned his attention back to the woman and reached out, slowly removing her glasses.

For a moment, the woman stared at them and both men hesitated. I saw the woman calmly take back the glasses and put them on. The thugs stepped back, away from her and made as though to sit down. The woman turned her head and looked towards the compartment door. As if it were a signal, the youths turned and almost ran back along the gangway towards me. Without so much as a glance in my direction, they threw open the door and stumbled into the next carriage, leaving the door open in their haste. I breathed a sigh of relief at their departure, slid the door shut and went to see if the woman was all right.

As I approached, she looked up and smiled as though she was aware that I meant her no harm.

"Are you all right?"

I felt like a chastened bystander who should have done more to help.

"Thank you. Yes. I have not been harmed."

Her complexion was fairly dark. African or Mediterranean, I thought, although there was no trace of a recognisable accent in her speech. She drew the dark head scarf close around her face in the manner of a nun's wimple, accentuating the shape of dreadlocks beneath it. I was amazed at the calmness in her voice after what I had just witnessed.

"Well... as long as you're sure," I said. I was not even sure myself that I could have done anything other than, perhaps, pull the communication cord and summon help if she *had* been harmed so I returned the smile and went back to my seat. As I did so, I could see through the window of the connecting door to where the two louts were now sitting quietly in the next compartment. I picked up my wallet and its scattered contents, wiping away the traces of lager on the sleeve of my ruined jacket.

Satisfied that nothing was missing, I found myself a seat that had not been touched by the deluge of lager. My mind was still occupied with the events of the last few minutes, and I soon started to drowse, faintly conscious of the train slowing, for the next station...

"Wake up, mate. End o' the line."

A tall, thin man with a broom and a plastic refuse sack was shaking my arm. I thanked him and, blinking myself awake, wished him 'Goodnight' and made my way out of the station into the chill Epping night.

It was not that I expected to see the woman again but, during the course of the following week, the incident played on my mind. Returning from my university class the following Wednesday, I actually found myself looking out for her. What was more disconcerting was my disappointment when there was no sign of her.

It took a surprisingly short time for me to settle to sleep until the thin man roused me again at the end of the line.

"You missed the excitement the other night,

mate," he said, cheerily.

I must have looked puzzled.

"Coupl'a young kids," he went on. "Couldn'a been more than about twenty. Found 'em stone dead when I went into the next carriage. Bit of a mystery accordin' to the Old Bill." He shrugged and laughed. "Drugs, if you ask me. Well, they're all round you nowadays."

I returned his grin and left him chuckling and shoving a pile of discarded newspapers into his sack.

There were large notices at the end of the platform and at the station exit asking for anyone with any information to come forward. The two youths had certainly been lively enough when they rushed past me. I couldn't see what help I could be, so I decided that the-powers-that-be would have to draw their own conclusions.

About a month passed before I saw the woman again. As she boarded the train, she looked casually in my direction and, without showing any sign of recognition, took the same seat as before.

I studied her reflection for a while and eventually dozed off.

The following week, a signal failure on the Central Line forced me to leave the train at the Bank station and travel by a specially-provided bus to Stratford from whence I could rejoin my normal route.

Being used to the relative peace and quiet of my regular late-night passage through Stratford. I was surprised by a commotion that seemed to have spilled over into the station from a nearby pub.

Then, as I rounded a corner on my way to the northbound Central Line platform. I saw the woman from the train a short distance ahead, apparently bidding farewell to another, similarly-dressed woman who then headed back towards the exit.

As I hurried past, apparently unnoticed, there was a sharp burst of laughter somewhere behind, accompanied by running footsteps which grew quickly in volume.

I turned and shouted a warning, just too late to prevent the nearer woman being bowled over by a group of hoodies who quickly ran off laughing.

As I hurried to offer assistance, her dark glasses skittered away on the tiled floor. Instantly, her hands flew up to cover her eyes as though she were blinded by the light.

As I leaned down to help her to her feet, she put one hand behind my head and pulled it firmly down so that her mouth was close to my ear. I heard her whisper frantically.

"My eyes. Look away. For your help and kindness, look away."

At first, I did not understand. Perhaps the woman was in shock.

I started to help her to her feet then, from behind me, a concerned voice called out "Stheno! Sister, are you hurt?"

"No, Euryale. Thanks to this young man, I am all right."

The names were immediately familiar to me and a desperate hope that I had misheard mingled with disbelief. But my trembling hand, brushing against her head scarf, confirmed the awful truth. There was movement under my fingers and I knew that I was not wrong.

The scarf fell away to reveal that the dreadlocks had bright eyes and darting tongues. Transfixed with horror, I knew what had befallen the two youths on the train.

From behind, a firm grip on my shoulder prevented me from looking round as the other Gorgon whispered close to my ear, "In the name of our mortal sister, Medusa, no-one must ever know." ♦

Guardian Angel

Albert put down his book with a sigh of frustration. Martha had never understood his interest in reading.

"Why you can't spend as much time doing something useful as you do with your nose in a book is beyond me," she nagged.

There was no point in Albert trying to explain yet again. She still wouldn't understand.

"Research?" she had scoffed, the first time he tried. "Rubbish."

Albert shuffled disconsolately upstairs to the bedroom. Changing into his gardening clothes, he left by the front door and made his way round to the back garden, avoiding Martha who was in the kitchen.

The early summer sun was warm and small wisps of cloud drifted slowly across the sky. But, to Albert who had always hated gardening, the breeze was too cold and mowing the lawn was a chore he could well have done without.

"And mind you do it properly," Martha shrilled from the kitchen.

Albert muttered an obscenity. He was dying for a cigarette. His giving up smoking had been another of Martha's daft ideas, like only eating health foods and not eating meat.

Reaching a point where he was hidden from the house, Albert squeezed between the potting shed and the fence at one corner of the garden. From a biscuit tin carefully concealed under the shed, he took cigarettes and matches. Within seconds he was savouring the delights of nicotine as a starving man greets a hearty meal. It was pure ecstasy.

Through a haze of contentment, Albert noticed something greenish-white in a corner beneath the shed.

"Mushrooms," he thought casually, dismissing the idea of telling Martha who had a passion for the revolting things. No. Do her good to go out early and pick them in the fields as usual. If she had a breath of sense in her, she'd buy them at the shop like anyone else. But not her. Oh, no. Twice a week, regular as clockwork. Sunday and Thursday. Up at the crack of dawn. The only way to be sure that they were free from harmful chemicals, so she said.

"Untouched by the hand of man," he remembered her saying.

He also remembered asking whether it was all right if they were kicked about by a load of monkeys.

After the row that had followed, she hadn't spoken to him for a week. It was glorious. He smiled at the memory and stubbed out his cigarette.

After lunch, Martha went for her usual Saturday afternoon shopping expedition. Thankfully, Albert went back to his book.

The story was quite good. He found it easy to sympathize with the leading character who was planning to murder his wife.

The thought set him daydreaming. For several seconds he imagined himself looking at a new gravestone bearing the name 'Martha Weems'.

Albert was jolted back by the reality of keys rattling in the front door. Clinging tight to the shattered remnants of his vision, he admitted to himself that he could no longer tolerate living with Martha. Getting rid of her, though, would be easier said than done.

"I expected you to have finished the lawn by the time I got back."

If there had been one shred of doubt left in Albert's mind, Martha's fate was decided by the sharpness of her own tongue.

Crouched in his hidden refuge, Albert pondered the problem over another surreptitious cigarette. Nothing violent, of course. Accident? Possible. Poison, perhaps?

Deep in thought, he studied the mushrooms he had seen earlier. There was a fully-grown specimen farther back in the shadows. They were almost identical to those to which Martha was so partial. Except... except for a bulge at the bottom of the stalk.

There was something vaguely familiar about that. Something he had read. Toadstool, he thought. Something 'cup'. No! 'Cap'. Yes. That was it! 'Death-cap'. He could hardly wait to finish the lawn and look it up.

The encyclopaedia entry was most encouraging. There was apparently no antidote to the 'Destroying Angel' as it was also known. Death from heart failure inevitably followed severe pain and convulsions lasting from eight to twenty-one days.

And the symptoms did not become apparent for about six hours. By then it was too late.

It was all too good to be true.

He slept little that night. This might be his only chance to be rid of Martha once and for all. He feigned sleep when she got up at first light.

As soon as the front door closed behind her, he dressed hastily and went into the garden. Selecting half a dozen toadstools, he took them into the kitchen and chopped them up ready to put into Martha's salad while she was getting ready to spend the day with her mother.

"Pity she always eats on the train," he thought wryly. "Her mother might like a taste as well. Then I'd be rid of both of them."

It was, as usual, a rush for Martha to catch the train. He did nothing to help in case she became suspicious.

He watched her gaunt figure hurrying away towards the station, content that he would soon be rid of her.

A leisurely breakfast of toast and coffee, then he decided to go back to bed and was soon catching up on the sleep that had evaded him the previous night.

He was startled into dizzy wakefulness by the telephone. He looked at the clock. It was just after two o'clock.

Martha's voice grated at the other end of the line.

Had she left her new gloves behind? If not, she must have lost them on the train and would have to have a new pair. He looked around. The gloves were lying on the hall stand.

So was the lunch box containing Martha's salad.

Albert wanted to be sick. He mumbled something to Martha about her gloves and hung up the receiver.

There was a sharp, cramp-like pain in his abdomen, then it was gone. Before he reached the door of the room, the pain came again—worse. He felt hot and giddy and his knees felt unable to support him.

He collapsed against the wall and slid to the floor, realising that, just as in all the stories he had read, something had gone wrong.

He struggled towards the phone, trying desperately to remember.

Of course! The toast!

He'd spread butter on it. But that had been a clean knife; he'd made sure of that. It must have been the kitchen worktop. Yes.

Stupid, stupid, stupid!

He'd forgotten to wash the place where the toadstools had been chopped up. The poison juices must have got onto the toast.

Another convulsion came as fear and darkness enveloped his mind.

What was that name? Destroying Angel? Guardian Angel more like.

"Martha's guardian angel! Damn her. The Devil looking after his own..." ♦

A Song After Silence

The soft click of the closing door was unmistakable.

In the semi-darkness, Mara's hand slid across the bed to taste the warmth of where he had lain. The movement caused the sheets to caress her naked body, reminding her of the tenderness of his touch.

It had been better than she had remembered.

Mara watched the shafts of light squeeze through a small gap in the curtains to sweep across the ceiling as cars passed in the street below.

So many years since Adam had left with that same soft click. The unexpectedness of his leaving had almost buried Mara under a crushing need to rebuild her world, to reshape her life.

How quickly, she thought, those years had passed. Total immersion in her work had left neither time nor place for personal relationships beyond the demands of business commitment. Now, that protective cloak had parted, allowing a single shaft of emotion to sweep across her carefully ordered world.

It would, she knew, be difficult to come to terms with the ease with which her defences had been breached.

It would be even more difficult to accept that it had been of her own choosing.

The constant strain of peering through driving spray at oncoming headlights had been accentuated by the incessant slap-slapping of the windscreen wipers.

A blue motorway exit sign loomed out of the murk. Mara had already passed the two-hundred-yard warning before she reacted.

Drawing into the exit slip without signalling, she felt the stiffness in her ankle as she lifted her foot from the accelerator and brought it down a little too hard on the brake.

Headlights flashed in the mirror and twin-tone horns blared scorn out of the darkness. She was grateful for the anonymity of rain-covered windows as a light blue Mercedes sped past and entered the junction roundabout.

Off the motorway there was little traffic. Mara mentally tossed a coin and chose the road taken by the Mercedes. She could see its indicator flashing as it turned into a filling station about a quarter of a mile ahead. Having filled up only a hundred miles back, she had no reason to risk confrontation with the driver who had just expressed such a poor opinion of her driving.

It was one thing to admit to herself that she had been a little... well... careless, but she'd be damned if she'd apologise.

The bright lights of the filling station dwindled in the mirror then vanished.

Soon, the road became a dual carriageway, and Mara followed a sign that indicated the nearest town.

The rain had stopped by the time she pulled into the car park alongside a modern hotel block. Quickly checking her appearance in the rear-view mirror, she retouched her faded lipstick and patted her short chestnut hair. Satisfied, she stepped out of the car into the newly-washed autumn night, shivering as the chill wind bit through her thin blouse.

Opening the rear door, she took out a silver-grey jacket. Shrugging it around her shoulders, she picked up her overnight bag from the back seat as the sound of tyres swished past on the wet tarmac. Careful not to step back, Mara slammed the door shut and pressed the remote locking button on her key fob. As she turned, the jacket was tugged from her shoulders. Her frantic grab at it sent the keys flying out of her hand. She clenched her teeth and hissed in annoyance as they skittered away and plopped into a drain.

"Not really your day, is it."

Mara looked round. The soft, well-educated voice belonged to a tall figure silhouetted against a lamp beneath which, she saw to her dismay, was parked the blue Mercedes.

She felt warmth rush to her cheeks.

"What's that supposed to mean?"

This really was too bad. Now, on top of everything else, she was about to get a lecture on the inadequacies of her driving.

The newcomer ignored the taunt and picked up the jacket. Then, digging his fingers into the narrow gap between the edge of the door and the bodywork, he prised apart the seal, teasing the material upwards and outwards until it was free.

"There we are," he said, examining the jacket. "Nothing a good sponge and press won't cure."

Mara was still waiting for the sarcasm to begin.

"I don't know what I'd have done without your help," she found herself saying. "Are you any good at rescuing damsels who've just dropped their keys down the drain?"

The man's face was clearly visible now and Mara saw it melt into a good-humoured, almost boyish smile. Then the smile changed to concern as a sudden, stronger gust of wind emptied teeming rain across the car park. He flung Mara's jacket around her, took her firmly by the elbow and ushered her towards the hotel entrance.

"First things first! Better get inside before

you catch your death...”

“But the keys...?” Mara started to protest.

“They’re not going anywhere.”

He bundled her firmly into the lobby.

“You just get yourself booked in and get out of those wet clothes as soon as you can. Leave the keys to me.”

He disappeared into the rainy night.

“Sorry, madam.”

The night porter took a white-tagged key from a pigeon-hole and placed it on the counter.

“Can’t do the bath. Only the one room left. Got a shower though. That do?”

It would have to. Mara had been looking forward to a nice hot soak. She picked up the key. No valeting service either. That was even worse. How on earth could she attend tomorrow’s board meeting looking as though she’d been dragged through a hedge backwards?

The room was adequately furnished in orange and white. A double bed, turned down ready for occupation, was flanked by shelves, one holding a white telephone, the other a radio alarm clock. In one corner, a television set stared blindly into the room, its empty screen reflecting the wall lights. By the window, a small writing table waited expectantly with a supply of headed notepaper. She hung the jacket over a chair and put her bag on the bed. Then, taking out her cell phone she dialled her secretary's home number.

"Hello, Janice," she said in response to a sleepy voice at the other end. "Sorry to wake you, but I've been held up. I may be a little late in the morning. Will you let Mr Ainsworthy know and ask him to take the Chair if I don't arrive in time for the start of the meeting."

She apologised again and hung up.

Sliding open the fitted wardrobe, she smiled at the row of softly chiming wire coat hangers and slid the door shut. If she'd had anything to hang on them, she thought, she'd have felt a lot better. But this evening's adventure had somehow slipped into her well-organised world without warning.

In the shower suite, Mara was pleased to find a coin-operated minibar. Beside it, a chair was piled high with clean, white towelling. She checked it. Two sets containing a bath sheet, a hand towel and a neatly folded shower robe.

She helped herself to a brandy, and turned on the shower.

The brandy was as warming as the steaming shower and Mara felt the long day's tensions float away with the cold of the rainy night. She turned off the shower just as there was a knock at the door.

"Who is it?" she called, hastily slipping into a robe.

"Your car keys, madam."

The keys! They'd completely slipped her mind.

Hugging the robe about her, she opened the door.

"Sorry. Took a bit longer than I thought."

It was the driver of the blue Mercedes. Water dripped from his clothes as he held out the keys.

The sight touched a chord that had eluded Mara for longer than she could remember. He looked so like a little boy who'd fallen into the goldfish pond. She smiled at the thought and took the keys.

"Oh, that is kind. Thank you so much. What can I say?"

"Glad to have been of service, Miss Langford." There was an air of forelock-touching in his delivery, but Mara felt that the words were genuinely meant. "I took a peep at the register while the porter wasn't looking." Then, seeing her puzzled expression, he added, "Your name. Mine's Miles. Goodnight."

Mara retained the memory of his soft brown eyes as she watched the tall figure striding towards the lift.

She saw him press the button then she remembered what the night porter had said.

"Miles. Wait."

She put up the door catch and padded along the corridor, as he looked back.

"Where do you think you're going like that? I know for a fact that there aren't any rooms left, and you can't go anywhere in that state."

"Oh, that's okay." He made light of his predicament. "I've got a change of clothes in the car. I'll be all right."

He turned to go as a melodic tone heralded the arrival of the lift.

Mara put a hand on his soggy sleeve.

"Well, at least bring your case up and you can change in my shower suite. Please. That's the very least I can do to thank you."

By the time he returned, Mara had tidied the shower. She let him in and sat on the bed with her legs tucked under her. She pointed with her half-finished drink towards a glass on the table.

"I hope brandy's all right. Works wonders on a cold night."

"Thanks." Miles slid his case onto the foot of the bed and unzipped it. Unfolding a dark blue suit, he straightened it on its hanger and hooked it over the wardrobe door handle. "How's your jacket?" He picked it up.

"Oh, I'll get it cleaned tomorrow. I've got a meeting at eleven. It'll have to do, I suppose."

"We'll have to see what we can do about that.

Cheers." He raised his glass towards Mara and took a sip from it. Folding the jacket carefully over his arm, he took it into the shower, reappearing a few minutes later with the mud and other marks sponged off.

Mara was surprised, not at the ease with which a total stranger had come into her life and established such a relaxed command of the situation, but at her willingness to encourage it.

"You'd better hurry up and change out of those wet things," she said. "Oh, sorry. That must have sounded awfully ungrateful. I mean I wouldn't want you to catch pneumonia. Why don't you take a shower?"

Miles finished his drink. "Thanks. I'll take you up on that."

There was something comforting about the sound of a man's voice humming above the hiss of the water.

The hurt that Adam had left behind all those years ago had all but vanished. Here in totally unfamiliar surroundings, and with a complete stranger, Mara felt the fullness of her womanhood returning. She blushed like a schoolgirl with her first crush, snuggling down to settle her head more comfortably on the pillow.

Slowly, the effects of the brandy and an overlong day engulfed her. The empty glass slipped from her fingers, tumbling from her hip to roll back and forth on the bed, finally settling against her thigh.

Barely aware that the sounds of the shower had ceased, Mara stirred as firm hands retrieved the glass from beneath her leg. She let her hand slide down until it touched his and, for a moment, felt the strength of his fingers entwined with hers, then it was gone. She opened her eyes.

"Sorry! Didn't mean to wake you."

Miles, now in a robe, was searching in his case.

"Shan't be long." He produced a small travelling iron. "Just going to see what I can do about your jacket before I go."

Mara leaned up onto one elbow and smiled. "Once a Boy Scout..."

"Not on your life. But I do travel a lot. And I once did a stint as a steward on a passenger liner."

He cleared the writing table then, deftly removing the television lead, plugged in the iron.

"Right! Now all we need is..." He slid open the wardrobe door. "Ah! Here we are. They usually have a spare at this time of year." He took down a blanket from the top shelf and spread it out over the table.

From beneath drooping eyelids, Mara saw

him pick up the jacket before sleep enclosed her again. She heard the faint chime of the coat hangers and felt the case being removed from the foot of the bed.

There was a shadow of sadness at the thought of his departure. Yet there was also a fear of waking; of learning that it was just a dream or, worse, of having to say goodbye. On such a short acquaintance, what other alternative could there be?

Gentle fingers brushed a tear from Mara's cheek, confirming the dream. She reached out and pulled him down beside her, feeling the warmth of his nakedness against hers. Every movement, every touch, every emotion that had lain dormant within her for so long came alive.

A song after silence.

The soft click of the closing door was unmistakable.

Mara watched the shafts of light squeeze through the small gap in the curtains to sweep across the ceiling as cars passed in the street below.

By the time she awoke, the sky was already bright. She drew back the curtains to let in the new day.

The rain had stopped, and the streets were already full. Mara's car stood alone, like a small island, away to one side. and the space beneath the lamp, where the Mercedes had been, was empty.

Mara's disappointment persisted long after she reached the motorway.

Years of self-imposed isolation, of resolution not to become involved, had crumbled. She was not ready for another relationship. Nor would she be until....

"Until what?" she said out loud.

Oh, why did men always make life so difficult?

No. That was unfair. Miles hadn't made life difficult. Quite the contrary, in fact. He'd rescued her from a very awkward situation. Damn it, he'd waited on her hand and foot. And without being asked. He'd taken command of the situation and asked for nothing in return.

Mara remembered the touch of his fingers on her cheek.

Hadn't that been asking? He had leaned across her and...

She had been drifting in that region between sleep and wakefulness, but she did remember him starting to pull the covers over her. It had been she who had reacted to the closeness of his body. Only then had he responded to her desire.

She was acutely aware of her inability to justify what had happened. He was, after all, a man and she, perhaps, just another conquest, but there had been a gentleness about him that denied her that belief.

Mara left the motorway and wound her way through heavy London traffic towards the office building. The uniformed commissionaire touched his cap in recognition as she entered.

In the privacy of the executive lift, she checked her appearance in the full-length mirror. It was immaculate. A far cry from the sorry mess of last evening.

"Oh, Miss Langford..." Janice came puffing along the corridor as the lift door opened. "I thought I'd missed you. A Mr Miles Boulton left this for you about an hour ago. He said you'd understand."

She held out a bulging manila envelope. Inside, Mara could feel the familiar shape of her cell phone. He must have picked it up by mistake. In her hurry she'd completely forgotten about it.

"One other thing, Miss Langford,"

Janice glanced down at a small business card.

"He asked if you'd care to dine with him tonight. He said there's a note in the envelope. What should I tell him?"

Mara ripped open the package.

Scrawled across a sheet of notepaper headed 'Boulton Shipping' were the words 'Pick you up at eight. Miles'.

Exasperation welled up inside Mara.

"Damn the man!" she thought. "He's doing it again. Taking command."

"Shall I tell him... 'yes'?"

Mara frowned.

"No," she said, firmly. "Tell him to... Oh... tell him to... make it seven-thirty." ♦

"I do hope you'll still be able to come on Sunday, Mr Stevens,"

Jed found it extremely difficult to keep his voice even.

"That's very civil of you, Parker. Particularly under the current circumstances. But I must say that I... and, of course, my dear wife... have been so looking forward to seeing your collection. I can't say how sorry I am about what has happened..."

Jed bit back his acrimony and hoped that it didn't show.

"That's OK," he said casually. "I always did fancy retiring a bit early so, well, where's the harm? Sorry business is so slack."

Then he added to himself, "You'll be all right. You've made your pile. It's poor sods like me who have to struggle to make ends meet. Twenty-two years and I get crapped on as soon as you have to give up a second biscuit with your afternoon tea. It must be really tough up there."

It was quite chilly by the time Jed arrived home. He went straight to the bedroom and grabbed a thick woolly jumper. Dumping it on a table in the kitchen, he opened the conservatory door, letting the rain-forest humidity flood over him, and drinking in the familiar odour of decay as he surveyed what he knew to be the world's finest collection of carnivorous plants.

The evening sun was already low in the sky and it cast long, eerie shadows across the rows of priceless specimens. Along one wall, a monotonous droning came from large incubator-like glass enclosures that seethed with myriads of entrapped insects of all kinds. Jed opened a drawer and took out a wide-mouthed syringe. He opened a bottle and let a single drop of syrupy fluid fall into the back of the syringe. Then, placing the nozzle to a sealed port in one of the incubators, he watched with obvious excitement as the insects scrambled frantically over one another to reached the sticky prize.

After a few moments, Jed closed the port and held the filled syringe up to the light. Satisfied, he walked up and down between the benches feeding writhing titbits to the waiting plants and muttering soothingly to each in turn.

"Not long now."

The evening ritual over, Jed went back into the now-cold kitchen and wrestled his way into the jumper. Filling the kettle, he lit the gas under it and went into the sitting room which was now in semi-darkness.

Jed flicked the light switch and a number

of spotlights focused on a large, shallow cupboard occupying most of one wall. Folding back the cupboard doors, Jed gazed lovingly upon dozens of tribal statues carved in wood or stone and arrayed on the narrow shelves inside.

Jed adjusted the position of one or two, aligning them so that the effect was of a subordinate entourage showing deference to the largest of the figures which stood proudly at the centre of the display.

Resisting the temptation to bow to the effigy, Jed switched off all the lights except the central one.

The figure's eyes seemed to transfix Jed, and he stood in silent observation until the whistling of the kettle dragged him back to reality.

Sunday, he thought, could not come quickly enough.

When it did, Jed rose early. He found it difficult to ignore the aura of hunger that emanated from the conservatory. In spite of unmistakable demands for his attention from all sides, he worked steadily on fulfilling the plan that had lived with him for so long.

Careful to remain out of reach of the hungry plants, he cleared an area on one of the rear benches and decorated it with leaves and bead ornaments.

At twelve o'clock precisely he carried the large effigy from its place in the sitting room and set it upon the newly made altar. The emanations of hunger were replaced by anticipation. They would, as Jed was well aware, be satiated very soon now.

The Stevens' were, not unexpectedly, about twenty minutes late.

"You might as well call me Henry now, Parker. Jed, isn't it? Wouldn't do to be too familiar as things used to be but... well...bit different now. Eh?"

He seemed to think that Jed had forgotten the way he'd been treated.

"Such a nice little place you've got here, Mr, um...?"

She was oblivious to anything that didn't jump up and wave a little flag at her.

"Silly bitch," thought Jed.

Tribal statues were obviously capable of waving little flags. No sooner had the Stevens' entered the sitting room than both went into raptures about Jed's collection. They were clearly knowledgeable on the subject of tribal customs and beliefs, particularly those of the southern hemisphere.

"I do hope you won't mind me saying this, Parker... er... Jed," Stevens puffed out his chest the way he had always done when he was about to air his usually-unwanted opinion. "There's one important item missing from your collection."

"Well, what do you know?" thought Jed. "He's noticed."

Then, aloud, "Oh yes, Henry?"

Stevens' chest puffed even further.

"A Tiki," he said airily. "New Zealand. Very powerful magic. Evil though. Difficult to get hold of, I dare say. Strange thing about those Johnnies, though. Did you know that they can only perform their evil magic by night at certain times...?"

"Oh, Henry!" Mrs jumped-up Stevens, cut him short. "You've told that story to dozens of people and ours has never done anything day or night since we've had it. It really has been a great disappointment."

"There is a very good reason, Mrs er..." Jed said quietly. "In New Zealand, it's dark at three o'clock in the morning—the hour at which they perform their magic. But when it's three o'clock in the morning down there, it's three o'clock in the afternoon here. The Tiki needs the dead of night to work his magic but our time is twelve hours out over here. Makes him quite safe, wouldn't you think?"

Henry's eyebrows shot up.

"Makes sense. Of course. Should have thought of that myself. Pity you haven't got one of the fella's since you know so much about them."

"Ah, but I have a surprise for you both. If you'd like to come through here, you'll find that my collection is much more complete than you think."

He escorted his excited visitors through the kitchen and into the suffocating heat of the mid-afternoon sun trapped in the conservatory.

"What I've done here," he ignored Mrs Er's obvious distaste of the atmosphere of decay. Won't bother her for long anyway, he thought. "Is to set the Tiki up in surroundings like those he would have been used to back home."

Henry studied the altar for a few moments before saying "Sounds as though you really believe in his powers, Parker."

Jed set aside the disdain in the comment.

"Of course," he said, "Don't you?"

The sun started to go behind a small cloud. Jed looked at his watch. Time to put the kettle on, he thought. He excused himself and left his visitors to gaze at the Tiki.

Jed closed the front door quietly and strolled to the local park where he mingled with the crowd of sightseers. The newspapers had forecast this celestial event perfectly. At two minutes to three, the moon started its transition of the sun's face. Thirty-two minutes later, the total solar eclipse was history.

Jed went back to the conservatory and returned the Tiki to its usual place then, filling the syringe with a large selection of titbits, he turned to face the replete plants.

"Afters, anyone?" he said. ♦

Figment

Lorraine was looking particularly desirable when I arrived at the office. The only few minutes we get to spend together is before patients start rolling in. But, today, there was someone waiting, though why he couldn't book an appointment like anyone else was beyond me.

I plonked two bouquets on Lorraine's desk.

"One's for you," I said, trying to hide my frustration.

Lorraine smiled prettily.

"And the other?"

"My wife. She thinks I've forgotten her birthday again. Give me two minutes, then send him in."

Straightening her white coat, Lorraine picked up the flowers and I went into the consulting room.

Tossing my briefcase onto a chair, I sat at the desk and let my anger subside. After all, it must be urgent. Nobody pays my sort of fee unless they really need help. I jabbed the intercom button.

"Right, Miss Prior."

Lorraine ushered in a man of smaller-than-average build which scarcely filled his grey trench coat. My impression was of a down-at-heel, ex-army type.

I got up to greet him and offer him a chair.

"Good morning, Mr... er...?"

"Sands. Harry Sands." He shook hands firmly.

"Doctor," he said, "I'm not sure that you can help me but..."

I put on a reassuring look and opened my notebook.

"That's not uncommon. So, if you'd just start at the beginning..."

He lowered his eyes for a moment then looked directly into mine.

"Doctor, is it possible to exist in two places at the same time? In the mind, I mean."

I considered the question for a few moments.

"Two places? Hmmm! 'In the mind', you say? Possible, I suppose. Two personalities, certainly."

"No. I don't mean schizophrenia, Doctor."

He was one step ahead.

"Look... say that a man—let's call him Smith—is a writer of fantastic stories. In real life he is imprisoned and charged with moral sabotage. He is sentenced to death for undermining the political structure of society by suggesting that there's a credible alternative to the harsh world in which he lives."

"But what...?"

I was quickly silenced by Sands' commanding hand.

"Sorry, Doctor. You need to appreciate the enormous stress under which Smith finds himself. Now, while he awaits execution, he discovers that he can find refuge in his fantasy worlds when he sleeps and—perhaps, inevitably—he escapes into one of them. His own world then seems to become just a figment of his imagination, but he is convinced that when he wakes up in his own world, he will be executed a few seconds later."

He paused.

"I mean... how can he tell if he's just remembering a particularly vivid nightmare or if he is really going to die?"

So, somewhere among all that gobbledygook was the real problem. I had often encountered the 'Smith' approach, and there was no doubt in my mind that he was actually describing his own fears.

"What name do you write under, Mr Sands?"

"It probably won't mean anything to you, Doctor," he said, apparently unsurprised at my conclusion. "but it's Narin Sandak."

It meant something all right. I'd tried one of his books recently, and I could understand why he needed to see a psychiatrist.

"And, of course, your leading character is this man Smith. Right?"

He smiled faintly.

"Well... no! I always write in the first person so he's actually Narin Sandak."

I made a note and looked at what I'd got. It wasn't much.

He needed to join a writers' circle, not to see a doctor. I was about to tell him so but then I remembered my fee. For that money, he was entitled to something. But, what?

"The point is, Doctor, if this is the dream world, I dare not sleep, because I know I'll be executed in the real world. But, if this is the real world..."

"Which, of course, it is..." Now, here was something about which I could advise him. "And that makes the solution very straightforward. For example, if you were run down by a car and killed, the entire world of Narin Sandak would end instantly since it exists only in your imagination. Here's another example..."

I slapped him hard across the face.

He gasped and drew back in surprise, throwing up his hands defensively.

"I'm sorry to have to do that, Mr Sands," I smiled reassuringly. "But the fact that you were not expecting it, and your obvious surprise, proves that it was not a figment of your imagination and, therefore, this must be the real world. So, all we have to do is to send you to sleep so that you can live out the final act in your nightmare."

Sands rubbed his cheek and nodded agreement.

"The imagination is far more powerful than any fiction," I went on, "but after death it ceases to exist. It stands to reason. So, once you have been 'executed' in your dream world, the nightmare will end. You can resume your writing with new characters and, hopefully, you'll avoid putting them in similar situations in the future."

Sands looked worried.

"But how can you be so sure, Doctor? You could be sending me to my death."

"Well, if we are just figments of your imagination, then we, too, would cease to exist when Narin Sandak dies in that other world. Do you honestly think that I would take that risk unless I were certain?"

I smiled reassuringly and asked Sands to lie on the couch. I called Lorraine in to assist me with the injection and we watched as the drug started to take effect.

The figure on the couch suddenly flickered and vanished and I knew Sands had been right!

I pulled Lorraine close and kissed her deeply, passionately.

At any moment now, Narin Sandak will die. When he does, my world... this world... the

world that exists only in his imagination... will
blink out of exist————. ◆

Home for Christmas

"Hello, Ted. You're early tonight. Come in to put a couple of extras away before the Christmas rush starts, eh?"

The landlord finished wiping a beer mug and hung it on the overhead rack. The old man ignored the friendly taunt and fumbled in his pocket for the remnants of his pension.

He slid a medley of coins across the bar.

"Just my usual," he said, then added: "And pint of best for my Tom. He's coming home for Christmas."

George filled a half-pint glass and set it down carefully.

"Best bitter, eh, Ted? Bit of a celebration, then. Been a few years since you've heard from Tom. Overseas, isn't he?"

"Italy, I think. Never been much of a letter writer, our Tom. Still, he gets about a bit. He was in Africa last time we heard from him."

George waved away the old man's money.

"On the house, Ted. Special occasion, this. Home for Christmas, eh? I'll bring the other over in a minute."

Ted nodded his thanks and headed for his usual table in a corner close to the log fire and sat down.

George put the glass on a tray and moved it aside to wipe the bar.

"Save your legs mate. I'm going that way."

A young man in a dark suit picked up the tray and took it over to the corner table where he slid onto the bench opposite Ted.

George watched as the two greeted each other and saw the young man take a small, flat box from his jacket pocket and slide it across the table. The old man opened it eagerly and examined the contents then looked at the young man with pride. He reached out and gripped the other's hand.

The young man smiled and withdrew the hand. He picked up his beer and raised it towards Ted then drained the mug in a few quick gulps. Ted took a drink from his own glass and signalled with it to George for a refill for the young man's mug.

"This is my Tom," he said, as the landlord placed a full glass of beer on the table. "Said he'd be home for Christmas, didn't I?"

George picked up the young man's empty glass and replaced it with the full one. The young man nodded his thanks, took a deep draught and pushed the glass away.

"Look, pop," he said quietly, "I've got to go now. But I will drop by and see you again." He placed one hand over the old man's.

Ted watched with moistening eyes as the young man withdrew his hand and edged out of his seat. There was a friendly "Cheers, mate," to George who watched as he left the bar and headed for the door.

"He's a real-life hero, my Tom."

George turned back to Ted. "Hero, eh? How's that then?"

Something metallic glinted dully in the light of the log fire as the other slowly opened the flat box and turned it towards him. The combination of purple and bronze was unmistakable.

George gasped.

"The Victoria Cross?" He almost whispered the words as Ted's fingers stroked the medal, caressing the words 'For Valour' embossed on it. "That young man who was just here? Whoever would have thought it? You must be very proud..."

Ted looked up, eyes bright, but said nothing.

George put the half empty glass on his tray and went back to the bar.

Just then, another customer came in, brushing snow from his heavy overcoat.

"Going to be a white Christmas by the look of it," he laughed, "I'll have the usual, please, George. Starting to settle out there. Half an inch thick already."

He took off the coat and hung it over the back of a chair.

George drew a double Scotch from the optic

and, placing it on the bar, leaned across conspiratorially.

"You'll never believe this, Jack, but that young lad's been awarded the VC."

Jack looked around the bar.

"Oh, yes? What young lad?" He drained his glass and ordered a refill.

"The one you just passed in the car park. Early twenties, dark suit. You must have seen him."

"Sorry, George. Didn't pass anybody in the car park." Jack went over to the lobby door and held it open "See for yourself."

The car park lights sparkled on a broad expanse of fresh snow that was already beginning to fill the single set of footprints marking Jack's own arrival.

George's expression changed to bewilderment. He looked across to where Ted still sat looking at the contents of the box.

"Well, I didn't imagine it," he said at last. "Ask Ted. It was his son, Tom. I spoke to him. He had a pint and a half of best bitter, then he left. Then Ted showed me the medal. He's over there looking at it now. Go and ask him if you don't believe me."

Jack smiled broadly. "Oh no. You don't catch me like that..."

George shrugged and leaned across the bar.

"Ted," he called to the old man. Then, to

Jack, "Straight up. I'm not joking. Really."

There was no reply from the old man. George called again. The old man was apparently too engrossed with the medal to hear.

"All right, then. I'll ask if it makes you feel better," Jack laughed, "Give me another of whatever he's drinking will you."

He picked up the drink and took it across to the old man's table. George watched as he started to sit down then suddenly bent over the old man. After a moment he turned and signalled to George.

"Better get a doctor," he said quietly as George approached.

"Can I help?"

The voice came from the direction of the bar door.

It was the young man in the dark suit.

"You?" George's jaw dropped. "It's your dad. I'm afraid... We think he's dead."

The young man's smile faded.

"Oh, I'm so sorry to hear that. Let me take a look at him. I'm Dr McReady's locum."

Later, as they watched the ambulance pull away, the young man asked, "But why on earth did you think he was my dad?"

"Because I heard you call him 'pop'," said George

"I see! Well, I'd arranged to meet someone

in the Public Bar but, as I was coming in, I saw him drop something in the car park. I picked it up and slipped it into my overcoat pocket. Well, my friend hadn't arrived, so I left my coat in the public bar and nipped through to return it to him."

"Nipped through?"

"Yes. Through the gents' loo from the other bar into the lobby"

Jack laughed.

"I must say we did wonder why you didn't leave any footprints in the snow when you left. George thought he'd seen a ghost."

"He wasn't the was the only one. This was still in my pocket, so I came back in to return it."

The young man spread out an age-brown newspaper cutting.

It was dated 1943.

Above a picture of a young man closely resembling himself were the words 'Posthumous VC for local hero'.

"It made him happy to think I was his son?" he said. "It is Christmas after all. and we could all use a ghost at some time." ♦

A Room for the Night

Michael switched off the engine and sat back in the driving seat with an exhausted sigh. He looked around the car park, surprised at the ease with which he had found a place at this time in the height of summer.

"Mind you," he muttered to himself as he released his seat belt and opened the car door, "I'll wager there won't be too many driving home tonight by the sound of it."

The sounds of revelry flowed across the car park on the still evening air, filling him with a hundred-mile thirst and an appetite to match.

He stood up and stretched just as the sound swelled momentarily and a young couple appeared from beneath a large neon sign that shouted, 'Welcome to Clancy's Bar'.

The sound retreated as the door swung shut.

The couple seemed oblivious to Michael as they headed towards a red open-topped sports car near the gate.

Michael pressed the remote locking button on his key ring, causing the indicators to flash and attracting the couple's attention.

"In the Name of Glory, will you look at that!"

The young man's expression was a picture, even at that distance. Michael watched as he grabbed the girl's arm and turned her around making her pregnancy obvious.

"Did you'se ever see the like?" He dragged the reluctant girl with him as he headed in Michael's direction. "Hey, mister, do you'se mind if I take a look at your motor?"

Michael felt a tinge of pride at the man's interest.

It was indeed a fine car and there were not many of its like on the roads. He had always gone for top-of-the-range models and this one was no exception. He stood back while the young man examined the vehicle from every angle.

"Sure, and 'tis a fine motor indeed," he said at last. "Did you'se get it from across the water? Ah, I see you did by the number plate."

He turned to leave then held out his hand.

"Now here's me with a lack of manners that'd shame me mother. I'm Sean Kelly and this is me wife, Eileen. We're just escaping from our anniversary party. Good luck to you, sir, and thank you'se."

Michael took the hand and smiled.

The red car roared off towards the next town. Michael watched until it turned the bend then pushed open the bar door. The air was filled with smoke and alcoholic laughter. One or two heads turned in his direction then away again. He ordered a half of Guinness and a sandwich.

"Can you fit me up with a room for the night?" he asked as the landlord carefully filled a glass and slid it across bar.

"I'm sorry, sir," came the reply, "you'll be needing to go into town for that, so you will. Your best bet would be the Ballydoyle Hotel. I'm sure they'll be able to help."

Michael nodded his thanks and looked around for a table. Finding none free, he moved along to the end of the bar, entered the cost in his notebook and slipped the receipt into his wallet.

Finishing his sandwich, he drained his glass and went out into the dusk.

According to the signpost, the next town was about seven miles away. Michael took out his mobile phone and dialled Directory Enquiries. There was only static. He shrugged. They'd said back at the office that coverage was poor in this area. Well, he'd have to wait until he arrived at the hotel to find out if they could accommodate him.

The road became less winding then stretched long and straight towards a bend about a mile ahead. He found it difficult to keep his speed down as the distance to the bend shortened.

As he entered the bend, a flash of red passed close to his wing. He braked, harder than he would have wished, and the car swerved violently. There was a grinding crunch as the driver of the red car lost control and it careered into the ditch.

Michael drew up and ran back to find the young couple from Clancy's Bar slumped in their seats. The young man stirred and groaned. He opened his eyes slowly and shook his head as though to clear it.

"Eileen!" He turned to the girl and gently gripped her arm. He looked up at Michael. "I think she's hurt bad. It's the babby, d'you see?"

"Is there a telephone nearby?" asked Michael.

"There is not. The nearest one's in town."

The girl started to make a snoring sound.

"I'll have to go for help, then," said Michael. "Look, take this. It's my card. I'm Michael O'Connor. When the police get here, tell them I went for help. I'll get back as soon as I can."

The other took the card and turned his attention back to the girl.

"And don't move her," Michael called back, remembering something he'd heard about making matters worse.

Ten minutes later Michael arrived at the police station in the main street of the small town.

"There's been an accident about two miles back along the road," he said breathlessly to the sergeant behind the desk. "And will you call an ambulance, too. There's a young girl been hurt."

"I will, so. And you'll need to be showing us where it is." The sergeant spoke into the radio that crackled on his lapel. He signalled to a colleague to take over at the desk. "If you wouldn't mind, sir, they're just bringing a car round. The ambulance has to come from Kilsaigh. It'll meet us there"

The journey back along the now-dark road beneath the flashing lights of the police car was quite eerie, Michael thought. Suddenly, he realised that they were travelling along the straight part of the road that lay beyond the bend.

"Wait!" He leaned forward and touched the driver's shoulder. "We must have passed them. It was at the bend back there. They must have slid further into the ditch and we've missed them."

Two minutes later, the car came to a halt at the point where the red sports car had gone off the road.

The sergeant and the driver got out and examined the area closely. After a few minutes, they came back.

"Right, sir. You'd better tell me what this is all about." The sergeant's tone was stern. "Would it be some kind of a joke you're playing, sir?"

Michael was just about to reply when the lights of an ambulance appeared, heading towards them at high speed along the straight road. It drew up alongside and the crew got out.

The sergeant spoke briefly to the crew and turned back to Michael.

"Well, the ambulance hasn't passed any accident, so I hope you've got a good explanation for this false alarm, Mr O'Connell. I think we'd better have a little chat back at the station."

"Why would I want to waste your time with a cock-and-bull story, sergeant? I've told you what happened..."

It was warm in the interview room. Michael slipped off his jacket and hung it over the back of his chair.

"You also said that you'd had half a pint of Guinness, yet there was no trace of it when we breathalysed you. How do you explain that?"

Michael took out his notebook. "Look," he said. "I always keep a tally of my expenses. See for yourself."

The sergeant took the book. He riffled through the pages and passed it back. "That doesn't prove anything."

"It's a sort of roadhouse about seven miles back. There was a party going on. Ask somebody who was there. They'll bear me out. Ask the landlord. He told me I could get a room at the Ballydoyle Hotel here in town. Wait a minute."

He suddenly remembered the sign over the door. "That's it. Yes. It's called Clancy's Bar."

The sergeant looked at him for several seconds then, without a word, got up and left the room. He returned a few minutes later with a tall, plain-clothed man who opened a manila file and asked Michael to go over the whole story again.

"And you say the couple introduced themselves. Why didn't you mention that before?" The tall man opened the file.

"I've only just remembered," said Michael. "The boy is Sean...er... Kelly and the girl's name is Eileen. Yes, that's it. Sean and Eileen Kelly. It was their anniversary party..."

The tall man seemed to be absorbed by the contents of the file.

"And what's the number of your car, sir?"

Michael didn't see the relevance of the question and said so.

"Would you just be answering the question, sir."

Michael told him, and the tall man closed the file and placed it on the table.

"Sergeant, would you ask the Superintendent to join us."

Michael caught his breath in astonishment when the Superintendent entered. The two stared at each other for several seconds.

The Superintendent was first to speak.

"It is you, so it is. Michael O'Connell. The man with the car," he said faintly, his eyes moistening. "And not a day older than you looked that terrible night twenty-five years ago. It was our first anniversary. Me wife, Eileen, died at the scene of the accident. They said if we'd got her to hospital sooner, she'd probably have been all right. You didn't cause the accident, but you never came back, and I blamed you for her death."

He sat down and put his hand on the younger man's arm.

"This is me son, Patrick. They managed to save him."

The young man took a business card from the folder and turned it over to show Michael's car number scribbled on the back.

"Me da used to tell me of the man who left me mother to die in a ditch. The car number didn't exist nor did the man's company. The police thought you must be on the run. I never knew Clancy's Bar. It was burnt down when I was only very small. And as for the Ballydoyle Hotel, well, we're sitting right where it used to be."

Michael was lost for words. For a moment,

the room spun. He looked blankly at the two men and wrestled with disbelief. Suddenly, instinctively, he looked at his watch.

"I'm so sorry," he said quietly, "But it's been an awfully long day and... I mean... I really think I should try and find a room for the night." ◆

Digital Farewell

"He did what?"

"He must be off his chump!"

"Anyone who watches the same clock for fifty years then asks for it as his retirement gift has to be a few coppers short of the full quid!"

Mr Rogers ignored the stage whispers and finished emptying his desk. When he had joined the company at fifteen nobody was called by their first name—still a company tradition. His first job had been to wind the clock that hung above the notice board where it could be seen by all.

Over the years, the routine of winding the clock and polishing its mahogany case had become a ritual that he would undoubtedly miss.

Now, as office manager, he was acutely aware of the derision that his dedication elicited from his colleagues, although seemingly appreciated by the Managing Director, Mr Anderson, whose predecessor had committed suicide following a financial scandal some twenty years ago. Indeed, had it not been for Mr Rogers' impeccable record keeping, the misappropriation of several particularly fine diamonds would never have been discovered.

A new clock now adorned the wall. Accurate to one second in a hundred million years, it was digital; silently marking off the passing seconds while displaying the date and the room temperature.

At a quarter to five precisely, Miss Gillacuddy, Mr Anderson's private secretary and, according to rumour, mistress placed a large gift-wrapped box on her desk and called for attention.

"Mr Anderson is abroad on business," she announced. "He has asked me to wish Mr Rogers well for his retirement and to hand him this cheque in grateful recognition of so many years of exceptional service."

She held out two envelopes; one sealed and the other open just enough for Mr Rogers to take in the number of zeroes. He almost felt guilty as Miss Gillacuddy sealed it and handed both to him.

Arriving home, Mr Rogers placed the envelopes on the mantelpiece while he prepared a pot of Earl Grey and a plate of crumpets.

Unpacking the clock, he placed it in an upright position on the sofa and studied it through a Bergamot-perfumed haze. He could not believe his luck.

For several minutes, he sat motionless. Then, laying the clock on its face, he carefully unscrewed the back of the case.

Rummaging inside, he produced a golf ball-sized chunk of modeling clay. He squidged it between his fingers then tossed it aside and plunged his hand back into the clock to grope frantically around until his fingers closed over a piece of folded paper. He opened it out to find a stark message printed across it in bold letters.

'THE CUPBOARD WAS BARE!'

An immense knot seemed suddenly to have formed in one of the crumpets he had just consumed, and sweat began to bead his brow.

He grabbed the letter from the mantelpiece and ripped it open, letting the cheque fall to the floor.

'Your asking for the clock set me thinking," he read. "Of course, no-one would ever think of looking inside it for the missing diamonds. It was really very clever of you to figure that out. No-one ever touched it but you.

'And, as for tying it in with the MD's casino win. Well, that was a stroke of genius. All the authorities needed was someone to blame and, once they'd found a suspect with reasonable opportunity *and* who had recently come into some money, they'd stop looking for the real culprit. But you'd figured *that* out, too.

'Genius! That's the only word for it. Sheer unadulterated genius! Your talents truly were wasted here. It was such a shame that he took it so badly. But then, that wasn't your fault. Well, not really.

'Of course, you could have taken the diamonds out at any time over the last twenty years and no-one the wiser, so you're probably a bit miffed about the way things have turned out. But, you really can't complain. No. I mean it! You really can't, can you? Well, not under the circumstances. Unless, of course...

'I understand Brixton is quite sought after these days. Well... some parts of it, anyway.

'So, there it is! And, thanks to you, I won't be back.'

The note was unsigned.

Mr Rogers swept up the cheque and peered at it as tears of frustration cascaded onto it, smudging the signature, 'Mickey Mouse', almost beyond recognition.

It was several minutes before he managed to focus on the PS.

'If I were you, I'd have a word with Miss Gillacuddy. She'll soon be looking for a shoulder to cry on, too. She was going to join me here but, somehow, I omitted to tell her where 'here' is. She made out the cheque, so she can't complain either.'

The words dripped with treacly sarcasm.

'But you always did have a soft spot for her. Go on, admit it. You know you did. Well, now you'll have years to commiserate with each other. So...

'Do enjoy your hard-earned retirement. I know I will!' ◆

Eight Days in Hell

(A 'true-life' drama)

Volcanic dust from Mont Pelée had rained down on the island of Martinique for two whole days, covering the town of Saint-Pierre and forming a thick layer in the prison yard. In the underground darkness of the condemned cell, Louis-Auguste Ciparis lay exhausted, his massive body cut and bruised by merciless beatings with pick handles and clubs by the prison guards.

The brutal treatment had stopped a day or so earlier, shortly after the prison governor had announced that there would be no reprieve. The execution was set for Thursday, May 8th, 1902, and fear of death had lately robbed Ciparis of his appetite as he now waited to die. He slept fitfully; his sleep constantly interrupted by the sounds of timber being delivered to the prison yard ready for the construction of the gallows which he knew was to bring his life to an abrupt end in just six days' time.

The only window was a barred grill set high in the cell wall. By grasping the bars and pulling himself up on tiptoe, Ciparis was able to see out into the yard just above ground level. On the morning of Saturday, May 3rd, he was awakened by the sounds of the other prisoners assembling for roll-call. Hoisting himself up, his despair deepened at the sight of the stack of timber in the far corner of the yard. He watched a group of prisoners building the gallows until, at noon, a whistle called them to the mess hall for lunch.

Hardly had they left the yard when the gallows platform became a pile of debris as another series of earth tremors from the awakening volcano shook the town. To Ciparis, it was an omen, suggesting that, after almost a month of imprisonment, there might still be hope.

The island of Martinique was in the throes of election fever and, despite the threat of imminent eruption, the danger to Saint-Pierre had become eclipsed by the tension of the political situation. Even Ciparis, a young Negro, convicted and condemned to death for killing a white man with a cutlass, was no more than a pawn in the game. The final word rested with Louis Mouttet, Governor of Martinique, whose decision would depend on his ability to turn it to political advantage.

Disregarding recent reports of deaths and of the impending danger from the volcano, Mouttet had ordered the local press to assure the people that there was no danger and encourage them to treat it as a grandstand view of Nature's pyrotechnics.

In his cell, Ciparis was awakened by the bells of the Cathedral of Saint-Pierre calling the faithful to Sunday worship. He listened intently, drinking in the sound, certain that he would be dead before they rang again. The next time would be on Thursday—Ascension Day—the day of his execution.

As he listened, he pictured his body in the crude coffin, covered with quicklime, and being buried ignominiously in an unmarked grave. He was praying for a miracle that might somehow save him when, suddenly, the bells stopped, and he became aware of a new sound coming from the cell blocks.

Quietly at first, then gradually louder, the other prisoners were protesting and smashing furniture to use as weapons. Fearful of the volcano, they were demanding to be transferred to the prison in Fort-de-France until the danger was past. The prison Governor knew that immediate steps must be taken to prevent the first ever prison riot in the island colony.

Within minutes, the sound of running boots was all around in the yard and musket fire echoed between the prison buildings. Ciparis crouched in terror as shots came far too close to the condemned cell. Muskets spoke again. Then again. Screams of pain as the bullets found their mark through the barred windows could be heard for several minutes until a loud voice barked out orders in the prison yard and silence fell.

Ciparis pulled himself up and looked out. He recognised the prison governor, a middle-aged, fat man who was not in the habit of wasting words. The riot must cease at once if the prisoners were to avoid dreadful reprisals: solitary confinement, withdrawal of all privileges, extra-hard labour and flogging with a six-tailed whip. The effect of such unprecedented threats was instantaneous. In the silence came the sound of bolts being drawn. Disconsolate lines of prisoners filed into the yard under armed guard. punishment of the did not commence until the.

The following day, Ciparis watched from his cell as each of the ringleaders was stripped naked, manacled to a plank set up in the yard, then mercilessly flogged and carried, barely conscious, to the solitary confinement block or direct to the prison mortuary, such was the severity of the flogging

It was during this Monday morning that two of the long-term prisoners–known as 'trusties'–came to his cell. They beat him with pick handles, saying that it was because of the trouble he had caused over the gallows. This, and a remark made by one guards regarding the dismantling of the gallows, once more fired the spark of hope although, when the wreckage of the gallows was removed next morning, Ciparis watched expecting to see more timber arrive. He stood on tiptoe at the grill, watching and waiting. But, by the end of the working day, no new timber had been brought, and his hopes rose again. Then, during the early evening, three trusties came to the cell to beat him senseless with the all-too-familiar pick handles.

As he regained consciousness, Ciparis heard one of them promise to make him suffer Hell even if he was going to be reprieved. Spent and broken by the beating, Ciparis offered up a fervent prayer, adding to an almost unrecognisable Twenty-Third Psalm the words: 'God bless the Governors', until exhaustion finally brought sleep.

Oblivious to the lightning that raged in Pelée's dust cloud and continuing earth tremors, Ciparis had a remarkable dream. In it, two men were discussing his fate, and one of them, the older of the two, said that Ciparis was not to die. The dream came at the very time that Governor Mouttet was taking that decision, in conversation with one Edouard L'Heurre, a man several years his junior.

It was nearly midday before the prison governor brought the news to Ciparis. But, although his dream had come true, he was to remain in the condemned cell until he could be transported to France where he would serve out the remainder of his sentence–a decision which was to write the name of Louis Auguste Ciparis in the pages of History.

The night of May 7th treated the townsfolk of St. Pierre to another magnificent display of fireworks from Mont Pelée. The morning of May 8th was bright and sunny, and the only signs of volcanic activity was a huge column of vapour and the ground that trembled before the wrath that was to come.

Shortly after five o'clock, the morning air was rent by the roar of the first stage in the final phase of the eruption. Smoke, the colour of blood, spewed from the crater, blackening the sky and filling the air with the smell of fear.

In his cell, Ciparis, choking with dust, took off his shirt, urinated on it, and draped it around his head for protection. Soon the dust had piled up outside the cell to such a depth that it blocked the grill, sealing Ciparis into an almost airtight box.

The final blast came in a manner which was hitherto unknown. The whole of the southern side of the mountain opened with a roar that was heard in Maracaibo, eight-hundred miles away. A great fiery cloud, travelling horizontally at fantastic speed, covered the five miles to Sainte-Pierre in two to three minutes. Within seconds the whole town was ablaze from end to end.

At two minutes past eight on the morning of May 8th, 1902, death had come to nearly thirty-thousand people in the town of Saint Pierre.

Despite their fears, the victims had been persuaded by the authorities that there was no danger. It was one of the most tragic mistakes in the history of Man. The cell block beneath which Ciparis was entombed, took the full force of the main blast and collapsed into a pile of rubble. The ash, which had sealed him in, now took most of the force of the scalding air as it roared through the grill, searing and tearing at his body until he wondered that he still lived.

From outside came agonized cries for help. Lifting himself painfully to the bars, Ciparis looked out. Of the prison—indeed, of the town itself—little remained.

Near the ruins of the cathedral lay scores of bodies, dead and dying, stripped of hair and clothing, while from every side came cries of "Help me. I'm on fire. I'm dying!"

Gradually, as death brought relief to their suffering, a terrible silence fell over the town and Ciparis was alone with his unanswered cries for help and the smell of his own burned flesh.

At the very time he was due to be hanged, Louis Auguste Ciparis had become the only survivor of the destruction of the town of Saint-Pierre, where 30,000 others died.

Incarcerated in the ruins, it was four days before Ciparis was found by a search party and taken, barely alive, to Le Morne-Rouge where he later recovered. His survival under such extreme circumstances was pronounced 'a miracle', and his sentence was suspended.

Such was his notoriety that people flocked to see Ciparis in a replica of the cell that had saved his life, when he became an exhibit in the famous Barnum and Bailey's Circus, where he remained until his death in 1929 at the age of 46.

Or... the circus let him go as public interest in his story waned, and he died a pauper on the streets of Panama in 1955 at the age of 72.

Take your pick and then read on...

I researched this story thoroughly, quite a few years ago, long before the Internet was invented. I submitted it to a popular weekly newspaper, and I was asked by the editor to provide my sources, so that the facts could be verified. Of course, I obliged.

Surprise, surprise, my story was immediately rejected, and a re-written version appeared in the paper a couple of months later. Same facts, same story – but with a staff by-line. Lesson learned.

Those readers who have access to the Internet might like to consider checking the accuracy of this story. They will find that a man, known variously as Louis-Auguste Ciparis (or Cyparis or Sylbaris or Cylbaris) did survive the eruption of Mont Pelée in 1902. He was a big man, sometimes known as Samson (or Sanson) because of his great strength. He was arrested and, either, sentenced to be hanged for the murder of a white man, whom he killed with a cutlass or, alternatively, sentenced to serve a month in jail in Saint-Pierre for wounding his friend with a cutlass during a drunken brawl.

In the latter version of the story, Ciparis escaped from custody and, unable to resist the temptation, spent the night at a local fiesta and gave himself up the following morning, so that he could complete his sentence. But, because of his escape, he was sentenced to eight days in solitary confinement, and it was his incarceration in this tiny cell that saved his life when the rest of the town's inhabitants died. ♦

The Truth Will Out

Whichever the version, Ciparis (billed as Ludger Sylbaris) did tour with Barnum and Bailey's Circus. Over the years, the reasons for his imprisonment became increasingly exaggerated, presumably to keep the punters rolling in. But, as with any such attraction, his notoriety waned, and audiences dwindled. Eventually, abandoned by the circus, he died in poverty in Panama in 1955.

But would it not be a poignant ending if the volcano really did decide to wipe out the town of Saint-Pierre at the precise moment that he had been sentenced to hang. Truly a miracle, indeed!

Other versions of this story are available, but the truth? That Ciparis did survive the eruption of Mont Pelée in 1902 and, later, joined Barnum and Bailey's Circus is not in doubt. And the rest?

The story has its roots in fact, but your guess is as good as mine.

Every one of the other stories above is obviously fictitious. That is to say – untrue. And it's much easier to make up your own 'facts' when you can't verify the truth, even on the Internet.

Which is why I prefer to write fiction! ♦

Meet the Author

Shortly after moving from south-east London to Kent in 1962, Bryan Darby's interest in writing was aroused when he met Peggy Cochrane, the well-known concert-pianist and composer and wife of 1930-40s bandleader, Jack Payne. It was this chance meeting that progressed to  a song-writing collaboration, to poetry and short stories, then, more recently, to stage plays.

As with most writers, he received dozens of rejections before his stories began to appear in the 'Evening News', a daily newspaper now, sadly, long defunct. Since then, his work has appeared in a wide range of publications across the market and, for more than fifteen years, he taught fiction writing at local Adult Education Centres.

During the 1970s, a good deal of his poetry was broadcast by the BBC, and it was one of these poems that inspired his first story, 'The Final Straw'. ◆

Early association with the amateur stage and several years working the Kent and Sussex Clubs as a singer and entertainer, lead naturally to writing for the stage. His works include:

Three-Quarter Moon
A creepy full-length thriller.

3m, 3f, 1m/f   120 mins.

Gold, Frankincense and Murder
**A full-length Murder Mystery,
suitable for any time of year.**

3m, 3f, 1m/f   90 mins.

Something to Hide
**A one-act Comedy
Particularly suitable for ladies' groups.**

5f, 1m/f   60 mins

For further information, or to read and/or download scripts, please visit the Publisher's web site at:

www.stagescripts.com

or ring:

UK: 0345 686 0611

Overseas: +44 700 581 0581